BENJAMIN HEDRICK'S TRUTH

Nancy Kirby West

CPCC

PRESS

A Division of Central Piedmont Community College

For Andy and Rebecca,
Love,
Nancy West

Published by
CPCC Press
PO Box 35009
Charlotte, NC 28235
www.cpcc.edu Keyword: Press
cpccpress@cpcc.edu

Cover Design by Susan Alford
Author photograph by First Choice Photographers

ISBN: 978-1-59494-038-5
Published and Printed in the United States of America
Printed and bound by Metrographics

CPCC Press is a division of Central Piedmont Community College.

To Robin and Tim for all the patience

and assistance they have given their Mother,

and to all who have been instrumental

in bringing a dream to reality.

Preface

Resemblance to persons, who once lived, the characters Benjamin and Mary Ellen Hedrick and those who were part of their lives, is not accidental. I have attempted to bring them to life-as I see them as a matter of justice and of historical importance.

As conflict over slavery arose to hysteria for slave owners and their northern opponent, the abolitionists, it is reassuring today to recognize that there were cool-headed and warm-hearted southerners who did not support slavocracy to the extent of disunion. These dissenters from the rushing tide, which led to the tragedy of the Civil War, have been largely buried under the events, which followed the triumph of violence.

Benjamin Hedrick is an outstanding example of the unheeded peacemakers in the decade before 1861. He was an early casualty of the war, losing the position on which he had planted his future and that of his family.

It was exciting to discover the wealth of material enfolding this story.

The letters are detailed and in particular descriptions of these lives; they are housed in the archives of the University of North Carolina at Chapel Hill and at Duke University. In addition to inventing some minor characters, I have used a novelist's license in editing these lively artifacts for clarity. Other documents are referenced, when not obvious by context, by chapter in the Endnotes.

Introduction

There are a great many rich possibilities to explain the genetic inheritance of John and Elizabeth Hedrick's first born, a blue-eyed son they named for Elizabeth's father Benjamin Sherwood. Davidson County, North Carolina, February 13, 1827: the place and time. No monument marks the spot, but the child grew into a man who made his mark.

The Sherwood background includes a William the Conqueror's standard-bearer who married Rowland Sherwood's daughter. The renowned philosopher-scientist Roger Bacon in his *Opus Tertium*. refers to the schoolman William Sherwood as a celebrated English scholar. John Sherwood who died in 1494 was the Bishop of Durham and Edward IV's legal advocate in Rome.

When the Sherwood's come to the New World, their tracks are clearer. First listed is "Thomas the Emigrant" who in April 1634 sailed from Ipswich on the ship *Francis*, captained by John Cutting. They anchored in Plymouth, no less.

But the antecedent of North Carolina Sherwood's is Francis who turns up in Maryland, taking the oath of fidelity to the Province on January 2, 1646. He was the father of Hugh Sherwood, born in 1632 and died in 1710 at his home "Huntington" in Miles River Neck, Talbot County, Annapolis, Maryland.

This Hugh was a prominent citizen, member of the House of Delegates and owner of several properties. His house, a mariner's cottage near the village of St. Michaels, is still to be seen, a listing on the National Registry of Historic Places. He and his wife Mary had eight children, among them Daniel and Hugh who were to move to Guilford County, North Carolina. Daniel and his wife Frances became the parents of Benjamin, our hero's grandfather. Daniel Sherwood is listed as a trustee of Pleasant Garden United Methodist Church, April 20, 1792.

Thus young Benjamin Sherwood Hedrick is known to come from an educated and industrious family. The influence of the Quaker community on Pleasant Garden is noted by Grandfather Sherwood in later writing, and by inference the same influence was felt by his daughter Elizabeth, her son's beloved teacher. This influence would have included antislavery sentiments since Pleasant Garden was a station of the Underground Railroad.

Along with his letters, young Benjamin would have absorbed the sense of justice which was to be so significant in his life.

When Benjamin Sherwood, the grandfather, was 20 years old, he married Sally Swaim and settled in Rowan County, an area which became Davidson County. In 1822, Benjamin was one of 35 men appointed Conscript Fathers by the General Assembly with the power to organize Davidson County. This group constituted the

Court of Common Pleas and Quarter Sessions when Davidson was formed in 1823. He also served as a Justice of the Peace.

It is clear that moving west twenty years later was a profound break with the community into which he was so well settled. His influence on his grandson was to resume in the 1850's after his namesake returned to North Carolina from Cambridge. His letters show him to be politically astute and happy in Iowa, a place not saddled with the burden of slavery.

Elizabeth Sherwood's brother, Michael Swaim Sherwood, also showed a thirst for justice and the initiative to act on it when, instead of following the family to Iowa , he remained in North Carolina and worked for the Manumission movement (a society dedicated to freeing slaves and helping them return to Africa). He was editor of the *Greensborough Patriot*, organ of the Manumission Society in North Carolina. He bought out his partner and became sole owner of the paper in 1854, just after his nephew Benjamin, the professor, returned to the state. The house built by Michael Swaim in 1849 can be still be visited in Greensboro at 426 West Friendly Avenue, another listing on the National Registry of Historic Places.

Now to the Hedrick side of Benjamin's family. John Leonard Hedrick, Benjamin's father, was of a German Lutheran family from Ulmet, Pfalz, Germany. Johann Peter Heydrich and his wife Milla, on the ship "*Robert and Alice*", arrived in Philadelphia September 11,

1738.

It was his son Johann Peter and his wife Margaret who settled in North Carolina, the area which became Davidson County. Around the year 1755, J. Peter laid claim to 1465 acres along "Four Mile Branch." This was the Hedrick kingdom from which Benjamin Hedrick's father John derived his inheritance, including the farm on which he and Elizabeth reared their family.

A monument was raised at the grave of Captain Johann Peter Hedrick in Beck's Reformed Church cemetery on the 200th anniversary of his birth. He was considered a hero of the Revolution, a story no doubt part of family oral history. The admiration and respect Benjamin held for the Founding Fathers would have been nurtured early in his life by hearing of his great-grandfather's heroism. His emotional response to the sight of Mount Vernon as described in a letter to Ellen may have its roots here.

The union of these two families- one English, one German- at the marriage of John Leonard Hedrick and Elizabeth Sherwood in 1826 brought together two distinct cultural heritages. It follows that their son Benjamin would become more than most, as his mother predicted.

The mother, into whose arms the baby was given, was a gentle, well-educated young woman. She was to nurture this son powerfully, giving him aspirations beyond the family environment. We know from his letters that he briefly attended a neighborhood school but that his mother was his teacher until he had the opportunity of going to school when he was twelve years old, stated in a letter to his grandfather. After bearing six more children, Elizabeth died in 1842 when Benjamin was fourteen years old.

Planted in this boy's early memory was a fearful sound, the clank of chains on the nearby river bridge. In his renowned "Defence" Benjamin refers to this:

> From North Carolina and Virginia nearly the entire increase of the slave population during the last twenty years has been sent off to the new States in the Southwest. In my boyhood I lived on one of the great thoroughfares (near Lock's Bridge on the Yadkin River) and have seen as many as 2,000 in a single day going South, mostly in the hands of speculators.

Obviously it was Elizabeth who planted the desire for more education, which burst forth one day, when he was a youth. After several years of working with his father in the fields and as a bricklayer, Benjamin, like the Prodigal Son, asked his father to give him his share of the property and let him go. Unlike the Prodigal, Benjamin wanted the means to pursue education, and he proceeded to accomplish his goal.

The Rev. Jesse Rankin, Presbyterian, held a Classical School, probably in his home, near Lexington. It was here that Benjamin came at age 19, to prepare for college. Boarding at the school, he was able, amazingly, to prepare for college in nineteen months. He entered the University of North Carolina as a sophomore in 1848 and was to graduate with highest honors in 1851.

After studying at Harvard, Benjamin returned to his Alma Mater as a professor. Thereafter, the traumatic development of his story.

Chapter One

Hillsborough Road
August 7, 1849

Although he was grateful to Governor Swain for a ride to Chapel Hill and the University from Hillsborough, Ben felt the trip might go on forever. The soft clop of the mule's feet and the burring of buggy wheels in the dust were lullabies to the tired young man who'd been traveling many hours in his heavy new suit. He was actually on his way to college. Delight smiled in his face.

Governor Swain had met him at the Hillsborough stage, as arranged by mail. Everyone knew to call him Governor, though he was President of the University. He had been governor at one time and would always get the title. Ben was fascinated by his ugliness, his big, loose-framed ugliness which made the first impressions, but was soon superseded by the simple friendliness he exuded. Maybe Ambassador of the University would be a better title.

Father would say Governor Swain drove like he meant to kill the mule. Fields and woods sped by. Ben secured his new hat and sighed happily to have his excitement matched by their speed. This trip to college was the beginning of everything.

Father and the children already seemed far away. Their home

by the big road was still vivid but seemed smaller as he recollected. He saw himself running to stand by the bridge as the slaves were driven over. The day dimmed a little as he remembered the bent backs and sad faces, the little children and women bringing up the rear. He heard them singing "Ride on King Jesus." His sympathy swelled again but then a hard jolt of the wagon brought him back to the present and the joy of moving on.

When Ben asked Governor Swain about his career, their traveling pace quickly dropped. The Governor loosed his grip on the reins and gave him a book of a reply. He said that like Ben, he had come from the country. He came from Buncombe, mountain country even more remote than Davidson County. Said he came to college at Chapel Hill for a while, and then decided to go directly into a law office to study for the bar. Said he went into state politics hoping to do something for the western part of the state and that he'd had to get the Constitution reformed to make a start on that. Said he was elected governor three times, back when the Assembly did the electing. Then he decided he wanted the job of heading the University.

Ol' Nate settled into a mild trot as the Governor hit his old courtroom stride, "The state needs leaders," he told his passenger whom he considered a bright-looking young fellow. "That's what this University is all about, and that's why I want to help her get off the ground, even if she is in the eastern part of the state. That Editor

Holden isn't the only one concerned about folks who don't have a lot of land. Our poor old Rip Van Winkle state is still trying to wake up and catch up. Some job, isn't it, Mr. Hedrick?"

Before Ben could reply, his driver continued to speak the flow of his thoughts. "Now, you were blessed to have a good school master in Mr. Rankin, makes you able to start out in the sophomore class. Lived right near you too, didn't he? Benjamin, if I may call you that. Education has long been one of our biggest needs here in the good ol' North State. Lots of children in country places are still growing up without a chance to learn to read or write."

"I know that, sir," Ben began to break in, "my mother was an educated woman and taught us our letters. Dead seven years now. I reckon I wouldn't be riding to college if she hadn't made me hungry for learning."

The Governor squinted down the road in a moment of respectful silence. He pointed to the grove beside the road. Scrubby rust-green thickets stretched as far as they could see on each side of the road. Then he said, "Right there you have an example of the need for education. Do you know what the cedars mean?"

"Yes sir, we have lots of overgrown land down my way. Means folks have moved away and left their land, moved out west most likely 'cause their land was worn out."

"Exactly. They didn't know how to rotate their crops to keep the land fertile, and so, there it is, wasted, probably cut through with gullies. You see, Benjamin, education is a practical thing."

Ben's eyes were blue sparks. College was going to be even better than he'd thought. "Well, Gov'ner, beside teaching us Greek and Latin, Mr. Rankin used to talk about scientific agriculture too. Had a certain kind of grass he thought could keep fields from washing."

And quickly, before the Governor could retrieve the podium, Ben added, "My grandfather, Mother's father, left for Iowa years ago, partly because of the worn-out land and wanting a new start. Packed up and took his family and all they had. We hear they're homesteading and raising good yields."

Lawyer Swain's courtroom instincts were roused. "You say your grandfather left partly because of the land. What were his other reasons?"

Deep woods had replaced cedar thickets. Ben stared into the dark trees and answered quickly, "To get away from slavery mostly. You see, Grandfather Sherwood was brought up with the Quakers in Guilford and doesn't go along with the notion of slavery. And he believes that slavery is holding back North Carolina and the whole South."

The Governor seemed to be clearing his throat of some really big obstacle. He finally got out, "Harrumph. Whoa, Mr. Hedrick. Now what you've said won't go any further, but I want to give you some important advice." He looked at the large gold watch he'd taken out of his pocket. "Now we've been on our journey most of an hour and jawing at each other most of the time. I like you very much, Benjamin, and expect great things of you as a student. But...and this is a firm warning...do not spout anti-slavery talk at Chapel Hill." He tightened his thin lips into a ruler.

"All right for your grandfather, he picked up and left, but for those of us planning to remain here, there must be no talk against the right of folks to own slaves. None. Too many toes would be stepped on -including toes of students' parents. There's just no use groaning about slavery here in eastern Carolina. Why, the big planters down by the coast... it's just not done! Why, the truth is, we can't even teach American history past the War of 1812 for fear of arousing discussions that could only lead to trouble." He stopped with the air of having stated irrefutable dogma.

Silence on the part of the new student in the dark blue suit. Then, "But..."

"There aren't any buts. And you're talking to a man who was in the audience, onstage as governor, in fact, when Judge Gaston gave his famous speech at graduation-'32, it was- against the institution of slavery. He got by with it, but those days were different from the present- still fear in the air after those Turner murders in Virginia, slaves killing white folks in their sleep. Since then the Northern

Abolitionists have started riding the subject for their hobbyhorse making the planters hang tight to what they've got. Better part of discretion to avoid the topic in polite society or any other."

The Governor's eyes recovered their twinkle. He tapped the serge covering Ben's left knee. "Tell you what, Benjamin Hedrick; I think you're going to eat up college."

Ahead on the right was a farmhouse, a pale cube simmering in the heat waves of the August afternoon. "Maybe we better stop here and get some water for Nate and ourselves, too. What do you think?"

"A good idea, Governor," Ben replied. His thoughts were circling overhead. Memories of the driven slaves, ragged and barefooted, the thud of their chains hitting Lock's Bridge were clear to this day, but they couldn't be shared. They were a wrapped package but leaking pain.

Miles ahead of Governor Swain's buggy, a farm wagon creaked along the narrow Hillsborough Road. It struggled up the long rise as it approached the village of Chapel Hill, which rode the crest like an ark in an exuberant tide of trees.

Mary Ellen Thompson could feel the rising and not just in the strain of her father's mule pulling uphill. She sat facing the rear of the wagon, her seat a kitchen chair. The parasol she held shielded from the August sun her newly pinned-up tawny hair and the face of delicate features including hazel eyes, which beamed vitality.

She reflected it was proper for a young woman old enough to put up her hair to ride apart from the driver, her Pa's elderly slave, Jack. Last summer she'd returned sitting in the seat beside him. Now she rode the chair like throne, thankful it was packed around with sacks of potatoes to keep it upright on the bumpy roads. Of course she wasn't yet too grand a lady to have helped load the vegetables, apples, and peaches for Ma's boarders.

She loved coming into Chapel Hill after weeks in the isolation of Pa's Rock Springs farm. Maybe you had to be a country-bred person to be so excited over coming into town. And just as the new season was starting at the college, it was even more exciting. Chapel Hill was like an old bear hibernating through the University's recess time but waking up and starting to dance when the students returned.

Ellen smoothed down the sleeve of her pink flowered muslin. The protection of her skin from the intense sunlight was essential if she was to be the desirable milky white-at least that's what Ma and all the other mothers told their daughters was necessary to attract young gallants.

Cam seemed to admire her entirely, especially her hair ("the color of pulled taffy").And she had found him attractive but had a nagging doubt about him. Had she really seen him coming from

Parney's cabin that night last spring? She had told no one of her suspicion.

Jack urged, "Come on, Amos. Giddyap." As they mounted the steep hill preceding Hillsborough Road's arrival at Franklin Street. They would turn into Ma's back lot just before Franklin. After five years Ellen was still highly pleased to be living on this corner. What with the college grounds running back from Franklin a few blocks down, the dry goods store, the churches, post office- the town was a wonder. She was home.

Strange, she thought, home was Ma's place, and Ma wasn't even her mother. Her mother's dear face appeared to her only in its tallow-white death mask now. But Ma was a reality. Pa had somehow persuaded their teacher, Eliza Jane Morrow, to marry him and mother his children along with him.

She had no idea why Pa and Ma lived apart, didn't even wonder anymore. In regard to Eliza J.'s powerful self, you didn't wonder, you just noticed and kept it to yourself. She laughed at her own thought that Eliza Jane Graves Morrow Thompson had never worried about keeping her skin milky white, and William, Ellen's Pa, was her third husband. Pa was just Pa. It was Selina, her stepsister, she was most anxious to see after three weeks in Rock Springs. She needed to hear what had been going on in town. With fall sessions starting, there was a lot to catch up on.

As they turned into Ma's, there was Willie, Ma's baby, playing under the magnolia with his sisters, Aide and Belle.

"Ellen!" Willie called and came running with the little girls. The three tried to jump up on the potatoes, but Ellen got herself down as quickly as she could. She hugged her half-brother and sisters affectionately while they all talked at once. It felt good to have the children hanging onto her skirt again.

Chapter Two

Chapel Hill

Gladness this morning as Ellen stepped off the back porch. Whoever that mockingbird was mocking had true pitch. Birdsong always touched her, and now the pure notes were almost too much to add to the warm summer air which seemed to relax her whole body. And there was the rich incense of the hedge bloom. I dramatize things, she told herself and changed her feelings into a prayer of thanks. She was especially thankful to have stopped grieving about not going back to Edgeworth Academy. She didn't have to give up her hopes of learning.

The shaded cool of the latticed well house was another delight. She cranked the windlass and drew up the muslin-covered pan containing butter for the boarders' table. Oh yes, the boarders.

Her short trim figure stepped more quickly back to the house than it had come out. The contrasting dimness of indoors halted her for a moment before she could really see the familiar scene. Like an altar, the fiery-hot stove was the center of action. Little Dumps was offering pieces of chicken to the iron skillet to be made into golden brown goodness. Her black face shone beneath a white head wrap as she turned to the table and added a crisp leg to the mounded platter. She would not fry very early in the day, as Ma suggested, since Little Dumps knew the fresher the better: she had her reputation to maintain among Chapel Hill cooks.

"U'm'm, that smells so good, Dumps," Ellen told her.

"Don't it, Miss Ellen!" Dumps answered, acting as pleased as if Ellen didn't always say that.

Ellen realized this was something she knew: everybody needs to be noticed; even if they're doing something they do every day.

"How many tables today, Ma?" she called when she had set the butter pan on the table's pocked tin surface.

Eliza J.'s bulk almost filled the pantry window as she stood before it filling the sugar bowls. She was wondering at the time about those fifty acres going for taxes next to Mr. Thompson's line. She always did the thinking for that sweet but silly man, her husband. It wasn't that he didn't mean well, he was just out of touch with anything bigger than getting the crops planted and cut. Ellen was asking about the tables.

Eliza turned. She was a robust woman with life in the palm of her hand. Her face was ruddy, her eyes had freckled irises and a tendency to narrow suspiciously. She wore a long apron at the hem of which showed the toes of William's work shoes - they seemed to fit. Her sleek thin hair suggested a man's since it was severely curtailed into a negligible knot. Not yet forty, Eliza had buried two husbands in the earth and a third in the country on his farm.

She focused on the dainty young woman before her. A flower face. A flower just coming into bloom, but she had spunk, Ellen did, and Eliza came as close to loving her as she did any other children about the place.

Eliza wasn't sentimental. Rumor had it that she'd given birth to some of her children between breakfast and dinner at the boardinghouse. When you serve fifty or sixty people every day in the week, you can't afford to take time out. Eliza didn't expect to be a mother again and thus didn't welcome Mr. Thompson for overnight visits in town.

"Ma?" Ellen deduced that her stepmother was planning some land deal while filling the sugar bowls. Eliza was a famous person in Orange County; her bossiness made Pa something of a laughingstock.

"Four. Half print on each table, Ellen. And none extra for that gallant of yours, Mr. Merriweather. Lots of our regulars will be back. First day of the term, you know."

"Yes, Ma'm." Always Ma'm to Eliza, never provoke that temper. Ellen picked up four white butter dishes. Sis Lina had already done her table setting; Ellen could tell from the low stack of thick white dinner plates left on the shelves.

Eliza turned with a tray holding the sugar bowls. "Will you set these out too, honey?" Her suspicious eyes grew soft. "I need to run over to the post office and get a money order. Graham's got a birthday coming while he's off visiting, you know."

They both knew she had just mentioned the child to whom she gave the most of her love. Her first-born to the late Mr. Morrow was the heir to all her hopes and dreams, the recipient of whatever largesse Eliza could garner from her cooking for students and her buying and selling of land. Ellen understands, Eliza thought, and then she said, "You're the same as my own, Ellen."

"Thank you, Ma," Ellen said.

The clump of heavy shoes accompanied Eliza out the back door.

The house seemed lighter with its engine out of the walls. Ellen hummed "Coming Through the Rye" as she went into the cooler front part of the house to set the butter and sugar around. Sis Lina had set ten places on each side and two at the ends, as usual. Belle and Aide, or one of them, had contributed a vase of bright zinnias to the near-center of the white cloth. She centered it. She liked things in order and looked around the table with satisfaction. She pulled the heavy draperies across the windows and wondered if they kept the heat in or out.

Then she went with her tray to the shorter table in the parlor and set down the butter and sugar. Sugar has a lid. Butter gets covered with a bowl to keep off the flies.

After returning to the kitchen for the other half of her load, she took it to the white-draped sawbuck tables in the back hall where faintly cooler air sifted through. These tables were recent additions.

"'Day, Miss Ellen," Parney greeted her. The dark face, much like her mother Little Dumps, gleamed with heat and her pregnancy bloomed under the long serving apron.

"Hey, Parney, how are you today?"

The girl smiled like a full moon. "Jes' fine. Sump'n good done happen, you want to know?"

'Sure, Parney, what's so good?"

"Well, Miss Ellen, it done jumped, jes' like my Mama say. This li'l critter done jump up and say, 'I'se here!'"

"That's wonderful, Parney. I reckon everything's going to be all right."

"Thank you, Miss Ellen. I hope you the same sometime."

"Yes, I hope me the same sometime, too, Parney," Ellen laughed and felt her face matching Parney's grin.

Sharp at noon the boarders came trooping from dormitories and classrooms. Professors and tutors came too - men away from their own hearths and tables and forced to pay money for their daily bread. Hungry, and glad to pay, most of them. They followed their empty stomachs to Mrs. Thompson's across the dust of tree-lined Franklin Street.

Ellen followed Parney who carried a large loaded tray to the hall tables. Ma'd been right, the tables were full. Many of the boys had that wall-eyed freshman look. Setting down a bowl of stewed corn, Ellen let her thumb touch the steaming stuff and cried out before she could stop herself.

Somebody's blue eyes seemed to say they hurt for her as she stuck her thumb in her mouth for comfort.

She slotted the young man straight from the country, but handsome. He was staring at her from his seat at the end of the bench. He looked away at her glance, but not before she had entered those eyes. They had welcomed her.

She smiled and said she was clumsy and that she was all right.

"You could have burned yourself," he said softly.

"Ellen, if you've recovered, meet my friend Mr. Benjamin Hedrick of Davidson County," Sidney called through a mouthful of chicken. He continued after swallowing. "Ben, meet Miss Ellen Thompson, one of our prettiest Presbyterians. She helps Eliza...Mrs. Thompson keep us from starving to death."

Ben rose as far as he could without the cooperation of his fellows and acknowledged the introduction. "Pleased to meet you, Miss Thompson," he said. He felt a lurch in his chest. He'd waited a long time to meet her. How dear a face.

He accepted some more corn atop an un-tasted portion. Parney grinned.

Back in the kitchen, Ellen asked Sis Lina, "What do you think of this new one?" Selina heard a new note of excitement in her stepsister's voice. She felt a stab of jealousy although she'd long suspected beautiful Ellen would have her pick of the boarders. Her own face was narrow like a hatchet, she thought, not a drawing card like Ellen's. She had to specialize in charm.

"Which do you mean? That scrawny one with pimples?" Lina teased. "Charming."

"No, you ninny." She didn't want Lina to know yet of the color tints and distant music surrounding the scene. "See the last one on the bench against the wall? Dark-haired, good-looking?"

"How can I tell if he's good-looking when he's bent over his plate so far he might drown in the gravy?"

"You see him all right, but don't forget, Selina Thompson, I saw him first." She sucked the burnt side of her thumb while feeling the beating of tiny hammers in her chest.

It was second-helping time. She brought freshly filled platters to the hall tables while Parney was serving apple brown betty to the dining room crowd. "You gentlemen have some more chicken? How 'bout some country ham?" She hoped her voice didn't betray that she'd like to serve herself to one of them.

Mr. Hedrick looked...how did he look? Like he'd eaten well but still might be looking for something.

Chapter Three

Chapel Hill
Spring, 1850

The students coveted invitations to Saturday night at the Thompsons'. The young men would arrive in the twilight since days were beginning to lengthen.

Mary Ellen, Sis Lina, Martha and their friend Mary Hooper sat on the front porch in rocking chairs trying to appear as if they'd lit there by happenstance, like dainty butterflies visiting the spot for a moment.

Did they talk and laugh a little louder than was proper? Did they peer across the road toward the college buildings? Inside did the dining room table appear strangely laden with teacakes and lemonade sufficient for a contingent of starving soldiers and their horses?

It was a kind of happiness, Ellen thought, to anticipate a few hours of company so keenly. Not sinful, surely. Though Ma wouldn't be downstairs; the clump of her shoes overhead was always a forceful reminder of the proprieties.

The breath of wisteria from the lattice at the ends of the porch stirred in Ellen a sharp delight in just being alive and being a woman. There was Cam and his appreciation of her as woman, his close-set eyes, his urgent kisses. She was a little afraid of Cam but excited too. And there was still the question of his visiting Parney for carnal purposes, as Governor Swain would say. Cam was just temporary in her life. She couldn't be a wife to such a gross man, even if the girls did tell her that plenty of men would satisfy their lust with slave girls if they could get by with it.

Parney's baby was almost certainly Cam's son, Ellen knew. After all, if Parney's husband, Aaron were his father would little Prospect have light tan skin and eyes set so close to his nose? Poor little baby, poor Parney, poor Aaron. "I don't even want to see that Cam," she said aloud suddenly.

"Why not, Ellen?" Sis Lina wanted to know. "He's got what this family needs - money. And if you were Mrs. Cameron Merriweather, you would be mistress of that big plantation with all those slaves."

"Well, aside from Cam - and I think you know why I don't want to see him - I would not like to have all those slaves. What a lot of cares a person would have! A boardinghouse isn't a patch on it!" she spoke emphatically.

"Do you really think so, Ellen?" Martha asked with a younger sister's eagerness to agree with her model.

Mary, who unfortunately resembled her father, that Greek professor with a long nose, joined in on Sis Lina's side. "Ellen, do you ever think of how sheltered we are here? Father said we don't really know what slavery is, compared to down on the big plantations. Why the Negroes here are just part of our families, almost. Look at Little Dumps and Aunt Juno here and Aunt Dilsey and Uncle Ike over at the Swains and Moses Horton - ever since I can remember the students have been paying him to turn out verses for their ladies."

"Oh Mary, what has Moses Horton got to do with whether I want to string Cam along? I admit this village isn't much of a slave-holding place, but I guess I'm trying to say I don't think I'd like to live where I'd have to see it on a big scale, let alone be responsible..."

Sis Lina let out a sibilant "Shhh. Let's change the subject, you all. Maybe the gallant in question won't even put in an appearance. She leaned out to look down the road, now blurred in the fading light. "I do see some fellow's a'comin. Surprise, Ellen, I think I see Little Blue Eyes leading the pack."

"I don't know whom you mean, Lina," Ellen said and her words met with laughter. A girl didn't want to be too obvious where her interest lay.

By that time the group of young men was close enough to be seen even in the dim light. The dark-haired slight young man two steps in front of the others felt he needn't guard his expression in the dark, and so he approached the Thompson's porch with eagerness all over him - in his eyes, his smiling lips, his quick step, and his swinging arms barely restrained from reaching out. His voice was tender as he stepped on the porch and greeted her, "Miss Ellen!"

She stood and walked toward him feeling she was moved by magnetism, yet she was in control of herself as never before. In both her hands she took the hand he held out.

Selina saw and heard the click of parts fit in the future of the young woman she loved like a real sister. Ellen would settle with Ben she knew, although she didn't know when. She didn't feel jealous either, she realized thankfully. It was like two creeks coming together to make a river - inevitable.

Ben wasn't sure of the outcome of his hopes that night. After all, what did he have to offer this popular and beautiful town girl? He had the goal of a career in science, some aspect of it. He was in love with science too, but he didn't plan to make a wife of her. He felt he was making progress in overcoming the shyness and awkwardness, which had been such heavy baggage when he arrived in Chapel Hill last summer.

"Let's go inside, it's almost dark," Ellen suggested as the four girls all were standing to meet the students. Martha, with her shy smile, stood back as Ellen and Ben led the way inside, followed by Sis Lina and sandy-haired Tom Price who didn't find her homely at all. Jeff Earnhardt, familiar as a boarder, was pleased to escort Miss Mary since her father's favor was much to be desired by a student of Greek. That left Martha with Louis Winget, two shy-smilers, well met.

Parney was lighting the candles on the piano as they entered the parlor. Ellen thanked her, and Parney bobbed and mumbled howdy in the general direction of the young folks. Parney didn't mind them, she wasn't bitter like Aaron, and she noticed quickly that He wasn't present. Thank you, Jesus, she breathed.

"How's your baby, Parney?" Ben asked the young black woman.

"He be doin' fine, sir," she said. A little embarrassed by the spotlight, she rolled her eyes toward Ellen for rescue.

"What's his name, Parney?" Tom asked as everyone settled onto the stiff parlor furniture.

She was backing out toward the kitchen, twisting her hands together under the long apron. "He be named Prospect, Mistah Tom."

Everyone listened and smiled. Jeff barked a short laugh.

Sis Lina remarked from her place on the horsehair sofa beside Tom, "I think it's a good name. It could be for Prospect Point, highest place in Chapel Hill, you know, or then it could be just for him to have a good chance in life, a good prospect."

"Thanky, Miss Lina," was Parney's parting remark, almost inaudible as she edged out of the room. It was good to have the baby, but she knew that was enough talk in the parlor about him. She wasn't meant to be the main show at the young white folk's party. And she didn't want to be asked to bring the baby in to be seen.

So far nothing had been said about the baby looking like his father, though it was mighty plain to Parney. Sort of tickled her too. Served that Mistah Cam right, buisting in on her the way he done. 'Course Aaron knew, knew and understood and was sorry for her and himself, too. She'd been afraid when he'd blown up the first time he'd got a good look at Possie's light color and little eyes settin' right close to his nose.

But Aaron had calmed down when she'd told him about that dark night when there was nobody on the place and that trash had come to her. Aaron had swallowed his fire, but she knew it still burned inside. A black man and a slave had no way to stand up to a white man, 'specially a rich white man. Less said the better. They'd still have their own children she knew, and she had reason to think it wouldn't be long. She had some fear of the way folks might judge the difference her babies were sure to have. Lord, help us, Parney prayed often. She closed the kitchen door and walked across the yard to her house.

Back in the parlor, Ellen asked, "Shall we start in singing?"

"You play, Ellen," Mary urged. "When you get tired, I'll take your place." Mary was sitting next to Mr. Earnhardt and not anxious to move to the piano stool. After all, not even Father wanted her to end up that terrible thing - an old maid. She felt a pleasant hum in her veins.

Everyone seemed to murmur agreement and stood to gather

around the piano. Ellen sat before the big square grand which filled half the room along with the Boston fern by the window.

Ellen chose a number and found the page. "Let's start out with "Hail, Columbia" and get your voices warmed up, all right?"

Ben loved singing with everyone in the candlelit room. He stood as close to the piano as he could decently, well, maybe it was a little indecent - the way he shoved Jeff out of the way. Tonight he felt bold and raised his voice to hail, "ye heroes, heaven born band."

Voices were well warmed up and in the middle of "Billy Boy" and his whereabouts when another young man burst in and jostled his way into the group, pushing Ben aside much more roughly than Ben had pushed Jeff.

"Look out, Cam," Ben said as the red-faced youth pushed Ben against Ellen's shoulder. Cam was drunk. What a smell he brought in with him!"

"Oh, where have you been, Billy boy, Billy boy? Oh, where have you been, darling Billy?"

Ellen continued to play and sing, and the other girls clustered close to her while the men formed a protective shield between them and Cam.

"What'n hell do you think you're doing?" Cam grumbled. He tried to push toward Ellen, got a hand on her back. Ben grabbed his wrist and pulled him around.

Cam wheeled, swung out with the other hand at Ben who quickly ducked away.

"Come on, Cam," Ben said. "You'd better go back to the dorm."

"Yes," Jeff chimed in, "looks like you've had enough party for one night."

The weaving student fell into a chair and sat scowling with a confused look on his face. "Don't you fellows try to mother me now, I won't stand for it," he warned.

"You can't stand for anything right now," Ben put in, thinking if he could just get Cam out, the party could be restored from the ruin caused by his intrusion.

Sitting seemed to bring out his need to speak, and Cam grew confidential. "Tell you what I'm going to do," he said looking around at the circle of wondering girls and angry boys. "I'll tell you right now, I'm no stranger to this Thompson place. Where's that li'l darky gal, what's her name - Parney? I know her real well. Fact is, I hear she's got a little chap looks a lot like ol' Cam."

A unified gasp from the girls helped get Ben into action. It also brought another young man from upstairs where he'd been visiting his mother Eliza J.

It was Graham Morrow, and Ben was glad to see him show up to help control the wild Cam. "Help me get him out of here, Graham," Ben told the taller man. "You heard what he said, didn't you?"

"Damn right he heard what I said," Cam ranted on, "and I'll say more. Got a plan to catch this pretty li'l Ellen and give her a baby looks like me too, only it'd be white. Now what do you stuffed shirts say to that?"

With Ben lifting one shoulder and Graham the other, Cam was propelled toward the door. Tom opened the door for the trio while Jeff and Louis stood protectively in front of the girls.

Ellen was speechless. She'd never heard such talk anywhere, let alone in her own house. That was that. She was relieved, in a way, to have the situation taken out of her hands. She wouldn't have to worry about Cam anymore. Rich or not, he was a bore. She was glad to realize Eliza J. had heard the whole thing and wouldn't have to have an explanation.

Martha and Sis Lina, white-faced, allowed their swains to seat them gently in the parlor chairs. Mary was still talking as she had been during the entire scene. "Well, I never...What an awful man!... Wait 'til Father hears about this!" were repeated several times by the professor's daughter. But her main fear was that Father mightn't let her come back to the Thompsons.

"Let's all go into the dining room," Ellen roused herself to say. "Just so we leave a little for Ben and Graham who've been such heroes."

After the heroes return and the departure of all the guests, Ellen and Selina were drowsing toward sleep in their bedroom upstairs. Ellen said, "He did the right thing, didn't he, Lina?"

"I'm sure you mean Brother Graham, don't you, Ellen?"

"You know that I don't. Mr. Hedrick, Benjamin, was such a gentleman. He wasn't going to stand for our being insulted by that gross person, Cam Merriweather. Weren't you grateful, Lina?"

"Yes, of course, and Ben was brave. Cam is so much bigger, he could have hurt him. Benjamin wasn't going to put up with that kind of talk about you, Ellen. He's in love with you, you know."

"I know," Ellen said. She smiled in the warm darkness, recalling something Sis Lina hadn't seen. Ben's lips were not only well formed but also very sweet.

Chapter Four

Chapel Hill
February,1851

Many more Saturday night parties, long sessions of studying, and long vacations at home were to pass before Ben could express the true condition of his heart.

On a September Sunday after that first kiss, he joined the Chapel Hill Presbyterian Church of which Ellen was a devout member. This step set him further apart from the Lutheran, farming, Hedricks of the river valley. There were no dogmatic differences that bothered him. How could God object to Ben's worshipping in the company of the woman he loved? Besides, as he had explained to his father over the summer, all the main people in Chapel Hill such as the Swains and the Phillips were Presbyterians.

Partly from fear that some other gallant would come between him and the woman he loved, Ben could restrain himself no longer. Many young men buzzed around the Thompsons, and Ellen was the prettiest of all the girls under the Eliza J.'s roof.

As it turned out, it was a Wednesday night in February when it happened. Wonder of wonders, Ellen and Ben had the parlor to themselves. The Mitchells were having a candy pulling which had attracted Selina and Henry and Martha, too. Eliza and Graham were visiting the Phillips, Eliza's little ones asleep upstairs, so the couple was alone.

Ellen, wearing her new deep red dress, sat in a rocker by a flickering lamp. She pretended attention to her "white sewing," drawn-work on ruffled pantalets. A simmering fire warmed the room. Ben was on the green velvet-covered loveseat, as close to her as he could get.

He was reading their favorite of Shakespeare's sonnets. Their happiness was such that whatever he read was like incense blending their eager feelings. It was Sonnet 27 that opened the way for Ben to declare himself. He blushed but his voice became firmer as he read the words expressing something of his state:

> Weary the toil; I haste me to my bed,
>
> The dear repose for limbs with travel tired;
>
> But then begins a journey in my head,
>
> To work my mind, when body's work's expired;
>
> For then my thoughts, from far where I abide,
>
> Intend a zealous pilgrimage to thee,
>
> And keep my drooping eyelids open wide,
>
> Looking on darkness which the blind do see:
>
> Save that my soul's imaginary sight
>
> Presents thy shadow to my sightless view

Which like a jewel hung in ghastly night,

Makes black night beauteous and her old face new.

Lo, thus by day my limbs, by night my mind,

For thee and for myself no quiet find.

The ticking pendulum of the clock above the mantel framed the silence. A log burned through and fell in two parts into the deep coals below. Ben stood dutifully to punch the log parts together and added one of the hickory logs from the wood box to rouse more flames. The little room was warm.

"Ellen, won't you put down that work and sit here beside me?" Ben pled as he took his seat again. "It's time for us to find some quiet by speaking.

Thank you, Lord, Shakespeare had helped. She quickly moved to accept Ben's invitation to join him on the loveseat.

Ben took her hand and stared into it as if the words he would speak written there. "Ellen, you know I love you, don't you? What the sonnet says is true, you are with me all the time." His blush was visible to her even in the soft light.

Her brilliant eyes signaled her feelings. "My dear Benjamin, I thought you'd never get out the words."

Their kiss was the deepest they had yet permitted themselves; in it was what could never be spoken. "I love you very much, dear, dear

Benjamin," she said as soon as she'd recovered her breath.

They released each other and sat staring into the fire. The feelings so long restrained crowded together urgently; both were a little breathless at reaching this new height.

Ben was conscious, as he always was when he was with Ellen, that he could easily wound her. But the tenderness in the rest of him made him quite fierce in restraining too much passion. After all, he must not frighten this delicate girl, his beloved.

But Ellen was a little frightened, even as she was almost weak with delight. She felt herself open like a flower and wondered if she would ever again be the person who had entered the parlor. The touch of his hand on the back of her neck seemed to make her close her eyes and open her mouth as if for food.

Then he suddenly stood up and turned away from her. "I think I had better leave now, sweetheart."

She stood beside him. "I hate for you to go, out into the cold, Benjamin, it's so wonderful to be together and say why."

"Yes, it is. By the way, did I ask you to marry me?"

She laughed her bubbling laugh of joy. "No, you didn't, but yes, I will. I think you're suppose to ask Father first."

"Oh, Ellen," he said and kissed her again as their bodies touched and then clung.

All the way back to the dorm, he laughed aloud and sang, "Oh don't you remember sweet Ellen, Ben Bolt". There, he lit a lamp and sat down in the cold to write his true love. He wrote on and on, blowing on his stiff fingers, saying what he had meant to say when they were together. "I was so confused this evening that scarcely a complete sentence escaped my lips."

He wrote that it wasn't in his character to put forth a declaration of love in honeyed words. He explained, as though she didn't know it, that he was reared in the country and so didn't know how to win a lady by flattery.

Then he proceeded to write for his true love's eyes the story of his life. He would give it her as a symbol of giving her his whole self. By the time he had finished, daylight was streaking into the room.

He folded the letter and put it on his desk.

When he read it over in the afternoon, it seemed childish, and so he decided not to give to her. He supposed he had been writing to help himself understand the momentous event after which he would never have just himself to consider.

Chapter Five

What a day! Ben felt the eruption of spring even more powerfully since he had learned something of the scientific view of the renewal he saw all around him. And maybe the solid, sandy colored college buildings soaking in the sunlight contrasted to make him even more aware of nature's fountain bubbling. Not only was there Ellen to love but also there were violets blooming underfoot and dogwoods unfolding their slow ivory green petals which would soon make umbrellas of snow over the campus and down Franklin Street.

He stopped and looked up, a silent tribute to the God they had just sung to in Chapel. Even the great oaks arching overhead were holding out transparent, rosy candles, which would soon become leaves. The Davie Poplar, there when the college was founded, had already leafed out. The blue of heaven was beyond.

With two hours free until geology class, Ben recalled what he'd planned to do with the time. On the way, he walked past his dormitory, Old East, and, as always, was reminded of Father. On the occasion of driving Ben back to college after vacation, John Hedrick has announced "Flemish Bond" as soon as he'd seen the building where Ben lived.

The bricklayer in John Hedrick had to admire the pattern of laying the brick which was rarely seen in the state. There was pride in his voice that meant John Hedrick knows a thing or two, these college people aren't the only smart ones. He hadn't cared as much about seeing Ben's room as he did about recognizing the walls. That had hurt Ben a little.

A drink at the well, center of living on campus, might bring me around, Ben thought. He stopped at the little shed which covered the source of the college's drinking water.

"Howdy, Jeff," he greeted the classmate who was pulling up the bucket at the moment. "How 'bout saving me some?"

"Well, I won't ask you what you mean." He grinned the grin of a committed, captured lover. "I'm too sly for you."

Jeff passed the dipper and gave Ben a big wink. "Aw, I don't have to fool with you, Ben. I'll hand it to you; you got yourself a fine little woman. Just beats me how such a sweetheart can live in the same house with Miz Eliza J.!" He looked at Ben with real puzzlement.

Ben swallowed some water and weighed his answer. "It's not so strange to me, Jeff. Ellen and her stepmother do live under the same roof, but remember, Eliza J. is only her stepmother, no blood kin."

"Well, I know that, Ben, and ain't none of my business, but it sure is a wonder Miss Mary Ellen got such a sweet way about her, growing up in that woman's house."

"You got Eliza wrong, Jeff, if it is any of your business."

Footsteps on the gravel path prevented the need of Ben's carrying further his defense of Mrs. Thompson.

"Well, anyhow, she sets a great table, don't she, Ben?" Jeff offered.

"Coming to the dorm?"

"No, I'm going to the Dialectic Library. I'll see you later on."

Professor Charles Phillips boomed "Howdy" and filled the shed with his commanding presence. He was abundant, in Ben's eyes - tall, broad of body, bright of complexion. Ben liked the man, judged him to be about ten years his senior, and knew him to be well versed in math and sciences. He'd even studied some at Princeton.

"This warm weather calls for plenty of water, doesn't it, Mr. Hedrick?" He threw the rest of the water Jeff had drawn on to the lawn, and began to lower the bucket by winding the windlass. This always reminded Ben of the farm and the long thirsty faces of Father's mules.

Taking the dipper of fresh water, Professor Phillips thanked him and then complimented him. "Mr. Hedrick, I believe in letting students know when they do well. You are the best mathematics student I have, about the best I've ever had. I'm going to miss you when you graduate."

Ben was thrilled. This was Crusty Charlie speaking. He thanked him as calmly as he could and inquired for Miss Laura and the children and for Miss Cornelia, his sister. Then, self-conscious, Ben hurried away with the explanation that he was off to the library.

Professor Phillips didn't have to know what he was going to do there. Besides, if he did know he'd tell Miss Cornie, and it would be all over the campus and the town.

Finding himself alone in the Di Library, Ben sat at the big table to think, to savor his high spirits and his nostalgia for home. He looked out at the beauty of the spring campus and was and realized how his world had grown since he left the farm and Father and the children - who weren't such children anymore.

Maybe he should feel guilty because he didn't miss them more than he did, didn't miss home. This was home now, the university where life fanned out before him like a peacock's tail - so promising, so expansive. His father's face, grim but dear, reminded him he wouldn't be here if Father hadn't offered him the chance to leave farming and bricklaying and come to college.

As a senior, he must look ahead and see what opportunities lay at hand for an educated man. And for a man who is planning to take a wife soon.

He was in this room right now because of Ellen and what she'd said Saturday night.

She said, "It just doesn't seem right, Mr. Hedrick. (She still called him Mr. Hedrick at times), for Parney and Aaron to have Cam

Merriweather's blind child - and he gets off so free. Not that I ever want to see him again. But it angers me every time I see Prospect trying to keep up with the other babies. What a name! Prospect! His prospects are so unlikely, aren't they?"

"You are right, my love. Slaves just don't have any prospects other than what their owners give them. I've always been bothered by the whole system, as I've told you," he answered her.

Before long they got into a delicious kiss again.

Suddenly he broke away exclaiming, "Judge Gaston!"

"What?" Ellen laughed that bubbling laugh until tears came into her eyes. "What does Judge Gaston have to do with us, please?"

He laughed too. "I don't know why, but he just came to me as you talked about Parney and her child." He tried to understand the connection while a strong wind caused the walls of the hold house to creak.

"All right," Ellen said, wiping her eyes with a dainty handkerchief. "You're too much for me, Mr. Hedrick. Are you doing an experiment of some kind?"

"No, no."

"Well, then, what is it? A lady doesn't like to have her courting interrupted by a judge." She blushed, much to Ben's enchantment.

"Oh Ellen, excuse me. It just came to me that I had meant to look up in the library the famous speech against slavery that Judge Gaston made to a graduating class - '32, I think Governor Swain said."

"I've heard of it too - from old Mrs. Phillips. She said if the judge hadn't been a trustee, there would have been a scene. Said he lit right into slave-owning, how it was wrong and holding the Old North State back."

"I didn't realize you knew about that speech, Ellen. Why didn't you tell me?"

"I didn't know you were interested. And I don't really know anymore about it anyway. I was three years old at the time, and now Judge Gaston's been dead seven or eight years, I reckon."

"Thanks honey," Ben said, putting her hand down after setting a kiss in its palm. "I'll hunt up that speech one of these days."

And he began to leave, an action expedited by the approach of Eliza J. The clump of her shoes on the stairs was a warning drum.

Ben stirred himself to action there in the Di Library. He rose and went to the bookshelves against the wall and found a shelf labeled "History of the University" and located the little volumes containing the reprints Judge Gaston's speech at graduation in 1832. The most recent printing was the fourth, so somebody must have an interest, he concluded. He read the speech through with rising incredulity, excitement, and assents. He reread the most striking part:

Disguise the truth as we may, throw the

blame where we will, it is slavery which more
than any other cause keeps us back in the
career of improvement. It stifles industry and
represses enterprise, it is fatal to economy and
providence, it discourages skill, it imperils our
strength as a community and poisons moral at
the fountainhead.

If Ben had felt buoyant on entering the library, he walked out feeling even taller, but also older. In a new way he was one with his past and those dark, sad faces running toward the river. And one with his present where Moses Horton was made a court jester and Parney a whore. Yet he also felt caution, knew he must keep this new integration a secret within himself, except for what he could share with Ellen.

It was true. Just as he had felt, just as Pastor Bennett had taught, just as many of the German neighbors in Davidson and Rowan likely felt, just as Grandfather Sherwood and his Quaker neighbors in Guildford had felt. Ben was part of a large group that reached back to Washington and Jefferson, men who knew in their bones, Ben thought, that it wasn't right or possible to own a human being. Even these great men had been caught up in the system.

Here now was the spirit of William Gaston, a man who had come often to the university not many years ago, a man who had been revered as a great judge and public servant. Here were his words lying like hot coals on the library shelf until someone would fan them.

But Governor Swain, all powerful here at the university world, had warned him at the beginning of his life here, not to speak against slavery. Ben had become a part of the silent conspiracy. Ben would carry the hot coals of knowing better but felt he wasn't likely to be the one to fan the flames. It wasn't a good feeling, made him look down at the path as he walked back across the campus. The sun-baked, many-scented place seemed to have faded a little, and he thought it would never look so innocent-bright again.

He still loved the University and was grateful for what he had gained from being there, but he felt shame and sorrow - as if he'd found his family was keeping an idiot in the closet. He believed that the University, including Governor Swain, whom he revered, was doing its part to keep the slave system by not allowing teaching or discussion of modern history. They were cozying up to the rich plantation owners, supporters, in turn, of the university.

As for himself, Ben felt he had a firmer grasp of his own convictions after reading Judge Gaston's words.

Without consciously deciding to go there, he found himself entering Old South and walking down the hall to Governor Swain's office. Maybe some guidance could be had there. Ben and the

Governor had become real friends, even though in the master/ disciple mode. Yet now, after the revelation in the library, Ben felt endowed with wisdom his master wasn't able to know even though, as governor, he had shared the platform when Judge Gaston made the powerful address.

The familiar high twangy voice called "Come in" in answer to his knock on the closed door of the office. But before Ben could pour forth the excitement foaming within him, Governor Swain leapt from his chair, dashed around the desk and enclosed the much smaller Ben in a bear hug.

Astonishment robbed the ready words from Ben's lips.

"Benjamin, my boy, you must be clairvoyant. Something in today's mail concerns you - that is if you want it to."

Could he never stop being a lawyer? Ben was overcome by the Governor's unusual show of enthusiasm to the point of speechlessness. When released, he sank into a chair facing the desk.

The Governor laughed happily and resumed his chair. "Well, Mr. Hedrick, I expect I've just about knocked you off your moorings. Let me explain, you deserve an explanation of my high jinks, my boy."

Ben's laugh was a little hollow as he attempted to appear nonchalant and perfectly accustomed to being assailed by the college president. He knew he couldn't pull this off when he heard his voice coming out small and childlike, "Well, you did surprise me, sir." Even

President Caldwell, from his portrait behind the desk, seemed to be listening for a revelation of some new truth.

Governor Swain's tongue moistened the full little lips to which his long nose pointed. The story began its slow emergence. "Well, you see, Benjamin, it beings to look as if someone may have hidden the silver cup in your bag, if you relate to my reference to the Book of Genesis."

"I hope that doesn't mean I'm going to be arrested, Governor."

Swain's eyes twinkled with pleasure at the retort.

"No, the connection breaks down there, but at least you can be a favored son. I'm going to tell you what I'm talking about and not tease you any longer."

At this Ben's blue eyes twinkled too, and he fancied President Caldwell smiled from his portrait.

"The letter I refer to, coming in today's mail, as I believe I indicated in my opening remarks, the letter came from Governor Graham - he's now Secretary of the Navy, you know, in Washington, a fine man and a good friend of the University. Now Mr. Hedrick, you may wonder what a letter from the Secretary of the Navy in Washington could have to do with you, Mister Benjamin Hedrick, Class of 1851." He stopped to breathe deeply, the picture of a man enjoying himself. Mr. Hedrick was registering astonishment very satisfactorily.

Mr. Hedrick was also perfectly silent.

"Harrumph. Well, the epistle under consideration relates to a position which Governor Graham is in a position to fill. It is a position for which I believe you, Mr. Hedrick, will be well qualified upon your graduation from this institution." He paused for effect, and feeling a little roguish, patted the paper on his desk. "All right, Mr. Hedrick?"

"I'm following you so far, sir," Ben managed to reply. His throat felt very dry, his heart raced as if he were standing an examination he hadn't prepared for well.

"Well, to come to the point..." The Governor paused again.

Ben hoped he would, and soon.

"Governor Graham writes that he hopes to appoint a qualified graduate of the University, one I would nominate, to the position of Secretary to the Director of the *Naval Almanac and Ephemeris*, the office of which is located in the town of Cambridge, Massachusetts, seat also of Harvard University and adjacent to the city of Boston." He stopped to allow the witness to respond.

"I'm overwhelmed, Governor. Are you saying you are going to offer my name for the position?"

"Understandable, my boy, harrumph, glad to be in the position to give you a leg up, so to speak, you have taken such good advantage of the opportunities here which I must admit are unexcelled in the South."

"We'll discuss the details later," he continued, "but Benjamin, I'm excited for you, as you can perhaps detect. And I've saved the best for last."

"What in the world?" Ben's question was sincere.

"Well, it is the Yankee world, but if I didn't think you could live up there and still remain a loyal Southerner, I wouldn't nominate you. You may recall, as I do, my advice to you as you arrived for the first time at this seat of learning, that success here is based partly on the avoidance of the topic of slavery. And if it was true then it is doubly so now and doubly so to a representative of the South and its institutions in the North."

"Let's see, Governor, you were going to tell me what you called the best part of the proposition..." Ben interrupted as Swain took a breath.

"Yes, that is, as a scientist, you would especially appreciate the *Almanac* position is a part-time one which would thus enable the individual holding it - if he chooses - time to attend lectures at the Lawrence Scientific School, a new department of the venerable Harvard University. What do you say to that, my boy?"

"I, I..." Tears sprang to Ben's eyes as he saw his path toward the future continue to rise and broaden. "Oh, Governor Swain, " he wiped his eyes furtively with the back of his hand. "You've guessed my fondest dream, and..." he swallowed hard, "you're making it come true."

Governor Swain had the tact to turn his eyes from the handsome young face to which they had been glued. He was very moved himself. Let no one say that David Swain had neglected to give assistance whenever possible to deserving students - sons of hard-working farmers not wealthy enough to be called planters, sons of such a man as Benjamin's father was, no doubt.

The clock in the hall boomed grandly. Its golden pendulum became a rejoicing tongue. The two sat as silence emerged from its reverberations. Then Ben stood as if propelled by a timed spring.

He smiled, grinned really, at the man behind the desk, reached for his hand and pumped it. "Oh, thank you, sir, I'll always be grateful."

"Yes, go my boy," he said grandly; then he added, "But you'd better keep this under your hat until nearer graduation - that is, until everything is officially confirmed. I exclude from the promise of silence a certain young lady whose future is involved also." Ellen was a favorite of the Governor's.

Ben sailed outside and felt for a moment that his light and happy frame might float straight up into the blue.

Passing the library, he recalled that something had happened there earlier, but he couldn't bring to mind just what it had been.

Chapter Six

The College
June 1851

Even though he wouldn't be present for graduation week and its ceremonies, Ben took great care in composing his senior oration. Knowing he was among the six taking First Honors made him even more intent to leave in the record a full statement of his philosophy at this time in his life. Then too, he felt quite responsible for producing an oration which would reflect credit on the University for choosing him to fill the position offered by Governor Graham.

After completing exams, he left by train for Cambridge, confident that he had done his best, that Ellen would not be embarrassed at the actual event when the speech would be read, and that he would receive his degree *in absentia*.

Commencement Week was festival time in the college and also the village year. Everything pointed to it. Most seniors had worked at their courses for four years. Some fathers, such as John Hedrick, had scrimped and saved to keep their sons' expenses covered; they were relieved the pinching was at an end. Other fathers who had paid with the greatest of ease were ready to bask in satisfaction as their sons received degrees from a safely Southern institution. The seniors' exuberance infected Chapel Hill and surroundings even as far as Hillsborough.

The great day was warm and cloudless by eleven in the morning when seniors, their families, faculty, and half the village strolled across the campus in the scent of magnolia and clematis bloom. Gerrard Hall was barely large enough when the crowd had packed in.

Ellen found the Commencement Exercises of the Class of 1851 hard to bear. She had dressed carefully in new sprigged muslin and topped her loped-up hair with a daisy, aware that she would be a target of scrutiny. Everyone knew she was suffering in Ben's absence; she tried, for Ben's sake, to bear patiently the uncomfortable feeling of being a public figure.

She could have recited his Oration if she had been asked. Instead she sat in the assembly, fanned, and tried to look cool while she perspired from the June heat and her own excitement.

When it was time, as shown on the program, Professor Phillips stood to read for Ben. "Felix qui potuit rerum congnocere causas," he boomed. Ellen knew the title meant, "Happy is he who knows the cause of things."

With the first sentence: "Bacon said man is the minister and interpreter of nature," she began a dialogue of response to her beloved's thoughts. She felt happy as he paid tribute to the Creator: "...all is perceived to be governed by laws as fixed as the great author himself." Good, my darling, we share faith in God, that's to build our home and family on. And yes, she was glad he went on to say, "...understanding nature is fulfilling the end of being as prescribed by the creator himself." Professor Phillips was reading with careful expression.

She came close to turning her head to frown in the direction of Pattie Battle whose sigh of either boredom or impatience had been quite audible from three rows back. You'd think some people could show consideration for others even if they themselves lacked the intelligence to understand what was being said. She stopped herself; such rash judging of pleasant bookish Pattie was wrong.

Of course if Ben hadn't been so deeply interested in science, Ellen herself probably wouldn't have known about Kepler, the astronomer and one of Ben's heroes. "His fame is co-existent with the globe he inhabited..." So everyone should know about Kepler, she concluded, knowing it wasn't likely.

The next part of the speech was one of her favorites as Ben listed the pleasures of being a Discoverer; he will "contribute to the wealth of body and mind, extend the boundaries of thought, and multiply the enjoyment of the senses." How blest she was to be engaged to the wonderful young man who had written all this. She had learned very much from him in addition to the enjoyment of the senses, which she blushed to recall in company; the teachers at Edgeworth would be glad about the advantage, which had come her way after she had abruptly left school. She lost the thread of the speech for a few minutes in the land of her own pleasant memories.

Oh, Ben. She longed for him so.

And he wasn't through telling all about the benefits a man of science can give the world. She nodded in anticipation as Phillips approached the conclusion, which she knew would make her heart dance with delight. Why wasn't everyone standing and applauding? Selina, next to Ellen, squeezed her sister's hand, seeing her excitement.

"Such are some of the benefits which a man of science may confer upon his race. And if his heart is tuned aright..." like yours, Ben dearest, "...will cause pulsations of joy in his own breast which only he who has felt them can rightly estimate."

The applause was rather long and loud as Professor Phillips took a little mock bow and looked straight at her. There should have been even more applause from those privileged to hear such a wonderful speech. Oh well, if Ben has been here to deliver it himself....

The next speaker was already underway, and Ellen's eyes glazed over when she considered how the poor fellow suffered when his looks were compared with Mr. Hedrick's. At least she could write to Ben that his was much the best speech and that it was well received.

Ben had told her that the title of his speech, "Happy is he who knows the cause of things" was ironic since he just could not say that he felt slavery was the cause of the negatives holding back the State and the country. And he was not happy to know the cause of this thing. He consoled himself that up North, people could speak freely about anything, including slavery.

At the social following the orations, Governor Swain came up to Ellen immediately to congratulate her on Ben's oration. "One of the best we've heard, Miss Ellen, but that's not surprising when we consider its author, is it?" Mrs. Battle, waiting to shake Swain's hand, rolled her eyes and might as well have said, "That's what you think."

Ma had been too busy to come to the Speaking, but Sis Lina stuck with Ellen. Her narrow face, broadened by a collar of starched ruching, was all smiles. It was as if she knew how much Ellen delighted in Mr. Hedrick's brilliance and also that Ellen needed support, as she was so conspicuous. Lina thought it did seem a little unfair of God to have given Ellen such a pretty face plus goodness and brains, considering he'd left off the beauty for Selina. Not that she begrudged dear Ellen a thing. God forgive me, she'll be going up North and no telling what will happen. She felt a motherly shudder of concern.

Then Tom Price was there saying, "Evenin' Mis' Lina. May I fetch you a cup of punch this warm evenin'?"

"Excuse me, Ellen," Selina said and walked away with Tom, her face as broad as a victorious smile could make it. She saw Mrs. Battle talking behind her fan with Mrs. Felter and deliberately wagged her bustle in what she hoped was a coquettish way.

The bald-headed, stocky man at the rear of the auditorium during the speeches wasn't recognized by many present for the occasion. David Swain had seen him and wondered what Billy Holden was doing there. But before Swain could speak to him after the exercises, Holden had slipped out. Just like him, snakes slip out. Then, he added to himself while getting punch for Eleanor, it wasn't strange for the editor of the NORTH CAROLINA STANDARD to cover Commencement. After all, not one of the struggling little colleges in the whole state held nearly as much interest for readers as the University. He knew he should try to overcome his dislike of the man, but it was hard, seeing he'd switched from Whig to Democrat when the price was right.

"Here you are, my dear." He handed his wife the cup. But after all- he concluded his internal debate- that was eight years ago, Holden's stuck that long with his second choice. He'd done pretty well considering he'd had to struggle hard for his education.

As she walked from the building with Tom and Lina, Ellen was on the second page of the letter she'd write when she got home.

Chapter Seven

Chapel Hill
June-September 1851

Deep in the Carolina woods, Chapel Hill was a world unto itself. But the outside world always seeped in with the arrival of the mail coach - the greatest event of the ordinary day. The post office on Henderson Street, around the corner from Franklin, was the center of interest. Here both townspeople and college people came to discover what the coach brought in the way of letters, magazines (*Harper's*, *Presbyterian Life*), and newspapers (Raleigh papers like the *North Carolina Standard* and *The Sentinel*; *The Greensborough Patriot*, the *Hillsborough Recorder*)._

For the Mitchells and the Phillips, and a few other natives of the North, there were the New York papers such as the *Times* or Greeley's *Tribune*.

As the slave-holding society gradually closed down on tolerance and stuffed the chinks against light from the outside, it could be observed that fewer *Tribunes* arrived from the North and more *Debow's Review* from New Orleans. The subscribers' changing choices mirrored fears that a threat to its established ways was rising outside the South. Some in the North just didn't understand the necessity for slavery, a large part of the region's wealth. Perhaps the defensiveness was more intense in North Carolina, a poor state clutching close what little it possessed.

As to every post office, those with most at stake came with highest hopes. Ellen was in this category as she walked down Franklin Street toward Henderson after seeing from home the coach struggle up Hillsborough Street. Would there be a letter from him? On this June beauty of a day, that was all that mattered. The arrival of a letter from Benjamin equaled a lovely day. Absence of a letter meant clouds and rain. She desperately needed to know that he had arrived safely in New York on his way to Cambridge...

Her need was met today by the sight of his familiar erratic handwriting on the blue envelope handed her at the window by a grinning Mr. Knowles.

She took her prize across to the deserted campus and found a bench behind one of the English gardener's new shrubs. She took time to use the letter opener she'd brought to slit the envelope, preserve the letter. She read:

> *United States Hotel*
> *Philadelphia, June 1, 1851*

My dear Ellen,

You as well as I will be somewhat disappointed when you see this letter written from Philadelphia instead of

New York, as I had promised. How this came about you will understand after reading the small journal of my travel which I will now give you.

I did not regret that I stayed so long with you that I had to travel late. Went to bed; slept three hours. Left Raleigh in the cars at four in the morning. This was my first experience in railroad traveling, and long will I remember it. The motion of the cars is slow and rough. But this would have been little had it been all.

About twelve o'clock we met with a broken-down train which had to be mended and then driven before us by our engine for six miles, at the rate of about three miles an hour. We got clear of this train, and the next thing that troubled us was to run off the track.

We got away as quickly as we could and hurried on to Gaston and got there too late for our connection. The cars that were to take us from Gaston had left a half hour before we arrived. So we had to stay at Gaston, it is one of the dirtiest, most uninteresting little holes I ever saw...

At Aquiria Break we went on board a very fine steamboat, the "Mount Vernon," and passed up the Potomac to Washington. This was exceedingly pleasant.

The Potomac is a beautiful river; sailing in a fine

steamboat was the way to have a perfect view of it. My feelings were much wrought by the beauty and sublimity of the river, the majesty of the steamboat moving on in unconscious might, the tolling of the bell. When I remembered George Washington and his deeds of patriotism as I stood on the top deck when we passed Mount Vernon, the unconscious tears sprang to my eyes. I felt proud that I belonged to the same country that received the services of so great a man...

I was sorry it was night, for it is a fine country, and I saw none of it. But I consoled myself that I would travel the same way, in the same direction, in company with one who would heighten every pleasure by sharing it, and remove all capacity for pain by her presence. May that time come soon.

We arrived here last night at one o'clock and put up at the U.S. Hotel where we will remain until tomorrow morning at six o'clock when we will leave in the cars for New York. I have seen and enjoyed more since I have been in Philadelphia than all of the rest of the trip - twenty times more. I am perfectly delighted with it, and if I had time I could write twenty sheets about what I have seen and heard today.

I wish so much that you could be here to enjoy it with me, for I know you would enjoy it. I cannot give you the faintest idea of what it is, I have never seen anything with which to compare it.

My love to you, my dear Ellen, and give my compliments to your Ma and Selina. I will write again when I get to Cambridge. Be cheerful. I am in fine health and spirits, and, believe me, your devoted lover.

BSH

Ellen walked home humming, the letter safe in her skirt pocket, a smile lighting her face.

A few days later, she was much bolstered to have another letter, more of a love letter, and one, which helped her to see her darling in his new situation.

Cambridge, June 5, 1851

My dear Ellen,

You will perceive by the caption on this letter that I have arrived at my port. I got into Boston this morning about six o'clock and am now snugly lodged in quarters assigned me by the Navy Department. I have two rooms, comfortable but small, on the third floor of the Nautical Almanac office. I have also a small office in which to discharge my clerkship.

My duties in the office will, I think, be very light and will last only five hours in the day - from nine to two o'clock and dinner is included in this time.

Lieutenant Davis is one of the finest and most gentleman-like men I ever met up with. Indeed I have found no one here but has treated me with the greatest politeness and even kindness.

This is a beautiful and pleasant place. I have the river, Boston, and the village in view from my window. But everything is so different from what I have been accustomed to that it will take me some time to appreciate the place aright. There is so much life and activity here that I don't know how anyone that is used to it could ever live in such a dull place as North Carolina. But still I hope that our old state may one day be as well or even better developed than this one is now.

I left Philadelphia Monday morning and in six hours was in New York. New York beats all for hubbub and bustle I ever saw. You never beheld ants around a large anthill more thickly or more constantly in motion than the people, omnibuses, drays, and all kind of vehicles in Broadway.

I stayed at West Point one day. Yesterday evening I went down to New York and left there at five on the steamboat "Knickerbocker" for Boston. We went the whole distance of 200 miles in thirteen hours. Part steamboat, the rest railroad.

I have seen and thought so much since I left you that it seems like it has been a month or two. I have thought of you many times, and you have been the constant companion of my dreams. And now when everything around me is as good as mortal need wish, a feeling of sadness comes over me when I think that you, who to satisfy me should be in my arms, are between six and seven hundred miles off.

This feeling will be much relieved when I shall read a letter from you and share your thoughts. I have thought several times of what you have probably been doing today. I suppose while I write this you are in the ballroom surrounded by the gay and thoughtless - or perhaps you are at home, weary from the fatigue of the day, but wherever you are, do you think of me?

Saturday evening sitting on the upper deck, sailing up the Long Island Sound, I saw a beautiful sunset. Over the waters I saw the moon calm as a sleeping maiden in the

distance and little sloops with their canvasses all spread
sweeping by at a steady rate urged by a gentle breeze.
With all this and much I cannot describe and our parting
scene fresh in mind, did I not think of you?

But my light is getting dim, almost burnt out so I
cannot see the lines of the paper, and besides, it's bedtime.
I will go then and see you in my dreams and wish that the
time may not be too long 'til I shall have you in my arms.
And this I shall wish for until I obtain it.

Give my regards to our common friends in Chapel
Hill and for yourself accept my purest and most devoted
love and believe me ever yours truly and sincerely.
Your absent lover,

    BSH

As she sat in the little parlor and mulled over this second
letter, Ellen tried to sort the mixture of feelings it aroused. She
heard in it a call to a place within her so deep it had not yet come
into being. Ben was calling her to come out of the enclosure in
which she had lived like a cocooned butterfly. There was some pain
in the stirring of furled wings.

"...everything is so different from what I've been accustomed to that it will take me some time to appreciate the place aright." (You're homesick, she translated.) "There's so much life and activity here..." She felt jealous for the country town of Chapel Hill where cows, pigs, and sometimes chickens wandered on the campus and in the main street. "...I don't know how anyone that is used to it could ever live in such a dull place as North Carolina is now." (You are always honest, even when it hurts. Could I ever fit into such a different place?)

Somehow the letters made their relationship more solid, enough so that in reply she dared refer to their engagement. She also passed on Ma's request that Ben buy her two quarts of clover seed and one quart of blue grass seed since the ones she bought here have been "no account."

A few days later she wrote that she was reading Wayland's *Moral Science* and found it quite sublime. She said of her God, "It seems I can never love Him enough." Ben was reminded that Ellen's short period of instruction at Edgeworth Seminary had given her a strong foundation in faith as well as literacy.

He replied, "...when I think that the same delightful thoughts are shared with you, I can do nothing but raise my soul in gratitude and thank God that he has given me so pure a being to love, and a heart that can love it as it deserves."

And the same letter went on to give her another kind of

consolation. "I have bought a very pretty gold watch with money my father gave me. It is a faithful little thing. I call it Ellen, and whenever I see it I think of you."

Ellen's heart was balmed that in this way Ben was keeping her steadily in mind, she was a regular part of his life at the North. And too, Ellen the Pocket watch was being worn close to the person of the one she loved so that she dreamed of feeling the pulse of his body as the little watch did now.

On August 20, Ben wrote in a way that gave Ellen special gratification. "*A very feast I have enjoyed today...You always know how to make me love you and to be in the good humor with myself and with everybody else...There was one thing which delighted me very much. You seemed to mingle thoughts with me...these thoughts penned and sent to you, when they come back to me, reflect your sweet self, then they are dear, they are precious to me. It seems they bond in sympathy between us. And though far from each other, we are for a moment in close communion.*"

In reply she wrote, "*My Dear Busy Bee, I have been alone much of the time in the little parlor where we spent so many pleasant evenings, and I trust will spend many more. I am sitting in it now, and in one of the most pleasant associations I am at the candlestick working on a bookmark or some other needlework and you on the other side entertaining me with Shakespeare, Burns, and a thousand other things.*"

In Cambridge, Ben's work with the stars took a practical turn. He wrote on September 26 that he had asked the Captain for an asteroid of his own. Tracking the ephemeris of this body would add $300 per year to his salary. This added income would, in time, be a boost to the household economy of Ben and Ellen.

On her side of their correspondence, Ellen tried to keep Ben up to date with happenings in the college and in the village. Chapel Hill wasn't really such a dull place, she would remind him. She told him of the times she ran into Governor Swain and how he always inquired about Mr. Hedrick. Some of the gentlemen of the senior class say whenever the Governor gives them a pattern; he always points to you and says, 'Look at what Mr. Hedrick is doing.'"

When she chanced to meet the burly Professor Phillips, she tensed herself for some teasing remark about her gallant. Professor Phillips had studied at Harvard too, scientific courses. It was he who was keen on learning about the lectures on geology Ben was hearing from the famous Swiss scientist Agassiz.

With the stew of life bubbling in her mind, Ellen took some time to linger at her desk when she had completed today's letter to Benjamin. She had the feeling that many of the faculty were leaning to overhear something of the superior academic life in which Ben was involved in Cambridge. She wondered if the Chapel Hill faculty thought of themselves as missionaries of the mind to the poor backwoods natives down here in North Carolina. The possibility didn't anger her, it was natural. They were mostly from the North themselves except for the Governor and the Battles.

But she felt that in the town generally there was a stronger leaning against things of the North and Yankees. She and Ben had talked about the South's need to defend slavery being a big reason for this pulling away, into itself. Things were continuing the same pattern. Holden's editorials in THE STANDARD were enough to fan anger against slaveholders if there were enough "poor whites" who could read his fuming.

Ellen had long thoughts. Most of the people she knew thought Holden went too far. He was a prophet of doom and had a bias against the University because he was self-educated, Governor Swain said. But then she knew Swain and his cohorts were still annoyed at Holden for switching from Whig to Democrat to get the job of editor of *The Standard*. Politics! She was glad Ben had no interest in the subject; he'd told her several times.

With Benjamin, it was science she had reason to be jealous of. How he loved to study it, especially mathematics. She felt he was sharing her sense of the stirring of unborn butterfly wings when he wrote that he was changing his main course from mathematics to chemistry, changing it with regret, she thought.

He wrote, "I shall be more successful with other sciences for the flirtation I have had with the old lady (mathematics). And while I could not confine life to the straight line, neither would I willingly choose the crooked line, but rather the graceful curve which is equally the pride of mathematics and the artist."

Sometimes he was too much for her; after all, she hadn't even finished at Edgeworth despite the pleas of her professors. With a forefinger she smoothed away the small frown she felt on her forehead. Nevermind, Benjamin was continuing her education. She delighted in whatever he wrote. If she didn't grasp it right away, she brooded over his meaning. She felt her face flush with the effort.

Chapter Eight

Rock Spring
October 11, 1851

"I reckon I'll go back to Chapel Hill, Pa," Ellen told him at breakfast. After all, she had been visiting at Rock Spring the whole second week of October.

He sighed to hear the tone of Eliza in his daughter's voice. But he knew he'd lost her anyway. Love and despair rolled together to make a sizable lump in his throat. Oh why had sweet Janie had to die and leave him?

"Whatever you want, honey, your ol' Pa wants you to be happy. Lord knows it's not very lively for you out here in the country, though I'd rather have it than all the dust and gab of town."

"You know I like Rock Spring, Pa, but I have been out here a week, and besides, the mail service is better in the village, you know that."

"Yes, Mary Ellen, I know your intended's letters don't come to Rock Spring." He squinted his little hazel eyes until they gave off a spark. "Can't come here if he don't address 'em here."

Her heart drooped for him. He felt rejected. "Now, Pa, Ben's afraid to send letters here for me because I might be back in town before they come. That's just the way it is."

Henry, wearing a teasing smirk, spoke up from across the table with its yellowed cloth. "Aw, Pa, there's just no way love's young dream can slow down." He winked at Ellen.

He had a piece of sausage stuck between his front teeth which were rather beaver-like anyway. He meant well, her little brother, even though she didn't need his help. She turned toward the kitchen and called, "Oh Harriet, how 'bout some hot grits?"

The breakfasters were quiet while the elderly black woman came in with the serving bowl and its curl of steam. She set it down before Ellen who thanked her.

Harriet was on her good behavior, they all knew. Ellen felt it had been good for Ma to scold the poor ol' thing, though she hoped she hadn't been too harsh. Out here in the country with almost no supervision, Harriet got careless and did things the easy way. Maybe Parney was having a good influence, too. In a way, Ellen regretted telling Eliza J. about the frying pan being used as a serving dish. She should have been brave enough to correct the cook herself, but Harriet was an older woman, even if she was a slave, and Ellen felt reluctant to call her down. Pa never would. He didn't notice much. But he'd been good-hearted to find a cabin out back for Aaron, Parney, and Prospect - to get them away from town.

He didn't want Ellen to know it, but William Thompson was glad, in a way, that Ellen was leaving. Now he could take a good glass of liquor whenever he wanted to, and nobody the wiser - except Harriet, and she didn't matter. It was something of a strain having Mary Ellen visit, but he owed her something.

"Do you like Prince, really, honey?" He felt happy at the recollection he'd given her the handsome gelding he'd traded off Grier.

Her round cheeks lifted as she smiled. Pa did love her and was as generous as he could afford to be. It was Ma who made most of the family living.

"He's beautiful, Pa, the nicest birthday present I've ever had!"

"Not every day a daughter turns twenty-two."

"Whew!" Henry whistled. "Ben came through just in time to keep us from having an old maid on our hands."

Poor Henry, Ellen thought, doesn't have a girl close to him yet, unless you count Selina. But you didn't count stepsisters, did you? Pa was waiting to hear more about Prince.

"I appreciate Prince so much, Pa. It will be so pleasant to drive him out on jaunts with my friends when we picnic." It was almost - and she felt bad even to think such a thing - as if Pa was trying to make up to her for sending her to live with his long-distance wife. He couldn't help it if his old farmland was worn out. She knew, too, it wasn't fair to contrast him with Ben who was making such a famous start in the bustling North.

While Pa and Henry sopped their biscuits in molasses, Ellen stared out the window at the overgrown boxwoods along the path. She let herself go where her feelings took her and ached for Ben. Life had lost flavor with him away - away at the other end of the world from Ellen who had never traveled further than Greensborough. The music that ran in her veins at Ben's touch was reduced to a hum after a separation of nearly five months. The hill of smoking white grits on her plate had developed a glassy glaze. She didn't want it now.

Pa wiped his mouth with his dingy napkin, sighed, and rose from the table. "Got to be out looking for those milk cows over on my new land, seems like they got through the fence last night." He raised his head to look at his children. "Reckon the Benton's land was worth the taxes?" He looked down at his hands, the picture of a modest achiever.

He needed still more petting. "Pa, you done good," Henry offered.

Ellen said, "You got a good buy. Hope the Bentons will have better fortune for themselves wherever they settle out west."

Pa stood clasping the back of the chair with both rough hands whose color reminded her of the yellow-gray soil he and his few slaves tried to work. "Well, I reckon they'll find richer land than we've got in these parts. I kinda admire their spunk, picking up and moving on."

"Aw, Pa, I kind of admire your spunk sticking it out," Ellen told him. "Mr. Hedrick says there is new hope for farmers because of what science has discovered about the soil." She should have held her tongue, she knew as soon as the words were out.

"I doubt it, Mary Ellen," her father replied, swallowing the anger that almost choked him. How in the hell could some highfaluting fellows shut up in a building figure how to make a field yield better? He didn't know and didn't plan on letting some citified professors tell him.

Ellen stood for her his kiss which was painful as usual due to the stabbing of whisker stubble. She knew her father's train of thought in regard to scientific agriculture, knew and understood. It was different when you lived in town. You learned there is a lot to learn. She knew she should be grateful to her father - and she was really - because he allowed her to live in the village and, for a while, even to go to Edgeworth to get more education. Poor Pa, he could hardly read and write himself, so naturally he couldn't grasp anything new.

She felt a joyous lurch of heart because her own world was continuing to open out because of that neat and handsome gentleman, Benjamin Sherwood Hedrick. She fought against the pride she felt knowing that as Mrs. Hedrick she would move with him into a bright new world.

"Thanks for coming to see your ol' Pa, hear?" His sheepish smile told her she had read him right, and he was embarrassed to be in conflict with her beloved. "You tell Mr. Hedrick I sent my howdy to him, and, Mary Ellen, honey, you come back and stay here with me whenever you take a notion."

His daughter was a downright pretty girl, a lot like her mother, with her fluffy hair and her little woman shape. Too pretty to be marrying a man who'll take her off to Yankee country, he felt. His eyes filled and stung. Then he remembered the others. "And tell the girls and Willie to come soon too. Oh and Miss Eliza, too, of course."

Pa looked pitiful standing there begging her to love him. She felt compassion. Her mother had worried about what he would do when she was gone, now the new life he'd taken on seemed to be held at a distance. How could Eliza do that to a man she loved, or had she married to get out of school teaching? It was hard to figure when all Ellen wanted was to be in the company of the man she loved. Dear Lord, please look after him, 'way up there with strangers, she prayed.

She smiled radiantly at Pa and both knew why. They hugged good-bye and walked arm-in-arm to the door. Then she watched while her father walked in his loping gait toward a field of cornstalks. His form soon disappeared into the skeletons of last summer's stand. Some ears like tapered scrolls of parchment still hung on.

The picture stayed with her a long time as Henry drove her home in the buggy. As they clacked down Buckhorn Road, she looked back to see Prince with his black coat growing dusty from the buggy's wheel cloud, tied and forced to trot to his new home.

The fall colors of the trees on either side of the road were red and yellow at their most intense. They might have been music with notes of fire and gold and the words were, "God saw that it was very good." But she couldn't tell any of that to Henry, it was Ben she needed.

It was corresponding with Ben that kept her alive through the fall and winter. In the letter he wrote from Cambridge on October 22, she got some news she was able to share with Corney.

> Chapel Hill
>
> *I suppose you have already heard of the Women's Rights Convention a few weeks ago in Worcester. I used to think all that was said about such things were mere nothings. But there are a number of persons now in Cambridge who went to the convention. The members and delegates were mostly of the peculiar class called sometimes "Old Maids." These individuals abound more at the North than at the South...*
>
> *Since my last letter I have been very closely engaged as usual, but my spirits have been good. I have had many pleasant thoughts, and in all of them, you, Ellen, were the soul.*

She lived for his letters, their assurance of his love and the fresh feeling of a new world opening for both of them. Both Corney and Sis Lina enjoyed hearing his comments on Women's Rights and there were more in his next letter.

> *It is morning and breakfast is over; and so I will go on with my letter. Everyone here is talking about politics which I don't interest myself with. Weather still continues cold. I do not go out often without an overcoat...*
>
> *When the Women's Rights Convention carries out its principles, the ladies will have as good a right as anyone to go "a courting," be lawyers, doctors, divines, professors, and everything they have a mind to. At the Convention in Worcester, the women made some big speeches, which have been published. There were some married women, either wives or widows. If the latter, they did not mention their husbands. Probably if they have any, they are rather small potatoes.*

She cherished all of his words, maybe especially the teasing ones which showed how closely they understood each other. Ellen was pleased about what Ben didn't dwell on, too. His comment about everybody talking politics and his not being interested was a good sign. From her occasional perusing the Phillips' New York papers, she was aware that Boston was a steaming abolitionist place. She prayed Ben would continue to stay clear of such dangerous thinking.

Chapter Nine

January, 1852
Naval Almanac Office
Cambridge, Massachusetts

Ben watched from the window of his office as Captain Davis walked down the street. Then he opened his desk drawer and took out a letter on paper already wearing thin at the folds. How terrible and yet how wonderful to be so much in love.

"My dear sir" indeed! He was her dear sir all right. He wasn't too keen on the part about Sis Lina entertaining in the parlor, the singing at the piano and all. Translated it meant some of the "gallants" had come over and enjoyed themselves with the Thompson girls and some of their friends. And Ellen had been there too enjoying herself no doubt and being looked at by the likes of Grant and Wheat and no telling who all. Maybe that fellow Vance the "irregular senior" from Buncombe was included. Ellen had written he was "very good-looking, witty, and fond of puns" - plus a favorite of the Governor.

It wasn't as if she wasn't betrothed. Anger stirred within him. How dare they spend an evening with his future bride with him so far away; she might forget she *was* spoken *for*.

He looked up from the disturbing part of the letter and stared blindly through the window glass. It still seemed something of a dream that he, Ben Hedrick, was at the *Naval Almanac* with this easy job. Maybe he'd exaggerated to Ellen about tracking stars when what he did was mostly paper work for Captain Davis. But it was true he had his own planet, Meta, as he'd written. He'd established its trajectory using new mathematical skills he'd learned from the renowned Professor Pierce of Harvard.

Well, he mused, it was only terrible and wonderful to be in love with Ellen of the pink cheeks, but it was also terrible and wonderful to be in love with Her Ladyship Science. This afternoon he would hear the famous botanist Asa Gray lecture at Harvard's Lawrence Scientific School. And it was so close by, not much of a walk to the old campus. He realized that back in Chapel Hill, Professors Mitchell and Phillips especially would envy him. And that they would have been horrified to hear Garrison last night, almost busting a blood vessel as he shouted about the wickedness of slavery. Maybe he was right that it is immoral, but I wouldn't dare let on I was impressed.

"Dream on, Mr. Hedrick."

That bold Van Vleck! Ben hoped he didn't blush and restrained himself from hurriedly slipping Ellen's letter into the drawer. He liked his Yankee co-worker, really.

"Never mind, John, don't tell me you don't do a little dreaming over letters from your Ellen."

John's eyes smiled behind his small round spectacles. "You're right, guess we're paddling the same boat."

Ben answered, "But you're blessed to be close to your lady. Why you just called on her last night, I'll bet my trajectory. Surely you won't begrudge me a second look at my distant Ellen's letter."

"Second?"

"Well, maybe a third look. You see, John, she's...special. I've got lots to learn about how she works before we marry.

"Never mind, Ben, old chap, you don't have to convince me. I'll be glad to testify to the southern belle that her intended is a faithful old dog."

"Would you now? I appreciate that, John. And now if you'll excuse me..."

"I'm going, I'm going." He shut the door quietly.

Rereading Ellen's words, Ben prayed thanks to the Father for the prospect of a future with this young woman and for the present when their love seemed almost visible fire, a new thing in the world being made of the powerful and tender feelings of Benjamin and Mary Ellen towards each other.

He whistled a few notes of "Ben Bolt," pocketed the letter and turned to his desk and the figures which awaited recording.

March 1852

How long the winter seemed to Ben. Growing up by the Yadkin

River, he was accustomed to brief periods of cold. In really cold weather at home, there were patterns of ice on the orange-red earth. Freezing temperature expanded the bright soil, almost like flowers of crystal threads. But these sights were short-lived, exciting almost.

Here in the north, he was not shocked by snowfall. Snow fell in the Yadkin Valley too, but what shocked the visitor to Massachusetts was how long the snow remained on the ground, on the streets. Rather than melting the next day and leaving soft sponginess underfoot, Yankee snow piled up and became a part of life for endless weeks, months even.

He felt a little nostalgic mentally transferring such an abundance of whiteness to his native countryside. How lovely on the rolling hills, dressing the pines and cedars in woods and thickets. And what fun the students at Chapel Hill would have. Snowball fights and sliding on frozen ponds would be a great temptation away from studies.

But here in Cambridge, where snow came to stay, it was taken for granted, loathed even, as it combined with the soot of town to become gray slush underfoot and under the wheels of coaches, drays, and trolleys. There was too much going on to permit a holiday spirit when snow fell.

He wondered what Ellen would think of the gray hanging-around part of northern snow. Probably accept it as he had. The two of them would have the same opinion of the snow and talk about it. No one here in his everyday routine found snow remarkable enough to even comment on, past a grumble or two about the need for rubber overshoes.

On the other hand, Ben was sure that the release of spring was going to be more spectacular in Cambridge and Boston than at home.

The middle of March found him still waiting to have the experience. There were some visible red tips on the elms and some of the other hardwoods on the campus, but the gray slush still lay over his view like a cold blanket. And many mornings still brought a fresh sheet of white to brighten the scene for a few hours.

It was the pure notes of the returning robin, which revived his faith one morning as he sat at his desk to write Ellen. Captain Davis was on a trip and not expected back until next Monday.

Settling into the letter, he wrote,

> I try to lay myself open to you as much as I can, but speaking on paper is not like speaking face-to-face. I know you cannot read my thoughts as I intend them in my letters. I have not even pleased myself, and I have not taken the pains I should, or I know I would never have vexed you or caused you the least anxiety. But when I have done so, nothing could be more pleasant than to know you will tell me of it. I have faults. When you see

them, do not be grieved too much but tell me.

You ought not to be so sad. I sent the first volume of Margaret Fuller's memoirs on Monday. I saw that Emerson wrote only part of the first volume, and that was what you wanted.

Maybe by the time you have read that, I shall be able to bring you the other volume - and in the mean time, I can read it myself. It is better than the one I sent. I do not much like Emerson's writing. But you will find the whole story stranger than fiction.

Margaret Fuller was a most wonderful woman. While she was living in Cambridge the people hardly knew what to think of her. They did not understand her. You will find the book is not in accordance with conventional thought, or do you and Corney tend to agree?...

I commenced to say you should not be so sad. The thought of leaving your old home need not make you unhappy... If God prospers us, we will be able to return sometimes and see them and thus renew from time to time the bands that from absence might be growing rusty.

If you are leaving one home it is to found another which will owe all its happiness to you. Will you not contribute cheerfully toward making a happy home? And *how would you make a happy home without marriage?*

He bit the end of his pen and stared at a cold-looking young tree standing with its feet in a plate of blackened snow. Maybe he wasn't putting enough sympathy in his letter. After all, Ellen would be like a young tree transplanted into a strange and colder space. He continued to write; the scratch of the nib was a low rasping sound in the small office.

> *I know it is natural for you to feel more anxiety than I at this time. All my anxiety was last year. I was then making up my mind what I should do. Then that I was agitated and anxious. I asked counsel from Him who alone is able to give it. My course was taken, and since that time I have been pursuing it as steadily as I have ability. To be wavering or hesitating now would seem like distrusting the goodness of God.*

> Good-bye, yours,
>
> *Benjamin*

Within two weeks he received her reply, which helped him to believe with certainty that spring was coming.

My dear Ben,

I thank you so much for sending me so soon the work for which I had written. I have been intending to tell you why I want it.

Miss Corney and I had a long chat about ladies in general and old maids in particular. We were trying to discover the reason why ladies of superior intellect who do not marry while young and who say they cannot find anyone worthy of them, should, after they have been Old Maids for several years, marry after all. And why they marry those who are far inferior to many who had offered themselves - as well as inferior to themselves.

We did not arrive at any conclusions which were satisfactory to both of us. Miss C. said it was because "all women are head and ears in their hearts 'till some fascinating youth has thrown his charms around it. They are in their youth so much occupied with head matters they have no time for heart affairs..."

It is very interesting work, so much of a higher life contained in it. Her talents were of the first order. I cannot, when reading, help wishing she had known the highest, the noblest life of man which is hidden in God his Savior. She does not seem to know a reconciled Father which it is my delight to feel. She only looks to the development of our powers and affections as the highest life in regard to a future life to come.

Wednesday, 5 p.m.

I would say more about Margaret but have something of more interest and deeper pleasure to communicate. I have just received yours of the 17th. I am not sad now. I am as cheerful as the sweet birds that carol their morning songs on the bough of the old oak that stands within the gate. I don't want to be sad and not tell you, nor do I want to make you sad by not telling you I am so. I am glad you know and trust so implicitly in the goodness of God and hope you never trust less and have cause to think differently of the decisions of last year.

Thursday morning

Is making others and ourselves happy the great object in life? Is that the way we most glorify our benevolent Creator? I am inclined to answer these questions in the affirmative, but I never took that view of life before. It is certainly worthy of him for whom and to whom are all things. He delights in making his creatures happy. Why would he have made us if he did not wish us to be so?

Then the great object of our existence is to live joyfully in the places where God has placed us and to reflect to the best of our powers the attributes of the Deity.

I wish your thoughts about these writings. I have some kind of aspirations for what seems to me to be a higher life, but it is slipping ground and filled with pitfalls and I often lose the way. I have been trying to settle in my own mind the highest and noblest work of a woman but cannot exactly make up my mind. I think I shall come to a wise decision when I think of it more.

When there is a thought in my letters that you do not understand, you will be good enough to excuse it. I always trust your love where there is something that is said that would have been better unsaid...

I am quite cheerful this morning, a little studious. "Be joyful."

Yours,

Ellen

That night with a full heart after receiving her letter, he wrote.

Cambridge, March 30, 1852

My dear Ellen,

Shall I go on and discuss the subject, which first made

you think of sending for the memoirs? I think I will not. You and Miss Corney can do better than I can, so I will wait and have your decision of the matter...

You wish to know my thoughts on the subject of making others and ourselves happy. I think that to increase the amount of happiness in the world is a bright and noble objective. The monkish notion that we must mortify our bodies in order to purify minds and render acceptable service to the Creator belongs more to the religion of Brahma and Vishnu than that which Christ came to teach...

But though in the main there is no better way to render service to the Creator than by diffusing joy in this world, there are cases which seem to be exceptions. The blessing was given to those who are persecuted for righteousness sake, or reviled and have all manner of evil said against them falsely. We may then also serve God by suffering for truth's sake.

Ellen carefully saved every letter that came from Ben. Years later she was to reflect that Ben must have had a presentiment about the way he would be called to serve the cause of truth. But no prophetic hint, other than rejoicing that their life together would include his thoughtful piety, came to her now.

When Professor Phillips wrote to Ben of the Professorship in engineering being announced at the University, Ben was immediately aware of implications for his future. Later in the year when the professorship was amplified into a separate department, threads of the Hedrick life pattern were falling into place.

But the great thing for now in both their lives was the approach of their wedding day. Ben wrote on April 21 that he planned to leave Boston May 27 and that he would stop in Washington to see Governor Graham, Secretary of the Navy and his benefactor in the *Naval Almanac* position.

She responded with plans made for the ceremony in the Presbyterian Church on Thursday, June 8. Professor (also Reverend) Charles Phillips would officiate. The wedding party would include Mr. Richardson with Sis Lina, Mr. Shober with Mae, Miss Corney, Mr.Norcome, and Mr. Wheat. Decorations would be by the ladies of the village.

The bridegroom was to arrive with - at Eliza's request - three pounds of fringed candies and three of stick candy "for setting off the table." And for "setting off the bride's table: two doves and a harp."

Ellen had known since April that her wedding ring would be of purest California gold, made to order and engraved with their initials and the year 1852.

She knew too that they would leave the following morning to visit Ben's family in Davidson County before leaving for the terribly distant town of Cambridge, Massachusetts.

Chapter Ten

Chapel Hill
June 3, 1852

Although the Presbyterian Church was only a block up Franklin Street from home, Eliza J. was determined that the bride should arrive properly in the family surrey. Brother Henry was instructed to act as a coachman and assist Ellen in her voluminous crinolines to enter and exit gracefully. Little Dumps' husband Oscar, wearing a tall black hat on loan from Dr. November, was in the driver's seat.

Ellen, an island in a frothy white sea of wedding gown, had the back seat to herself. She felt quite set apart today anyway and worthy to be fussed over by Ma and Sis Lina who had installed her carefully to minimize wrinkling.

As departure time approached, Ma leaned in toward her so that for a moment she appeared to have bangs of surrey fringe. "You are a beautiful bride, my dear," Ma sniffed, looking unexpectedly stricken. She pulled away quickly. Pa put his hand in and squeezed Ellen's.

Selina, decked in pink peau de soie, called, "Pull that ruching a little further back on your head." She held her hands beneath the fragrant crown of creamy roses, the feverfew and fern which she would place on the bride's head before the walk down the aisle. "You are the most beautiful bride I've ever seen. That Mr. Hedrick is one fortunate man." She wished she could think of something special to say, it was such a special moment. She expected being so excited had probably brought good color to her cheeks and that Mr. Richardson would probably notice.

When the surrey had pulled away, Ma, Pa and Selina began walking toward the church. The girls and Willie had already gone; they had said four-thirty was close enough to five o'clock and besides the flowers might need a little more water. They were proud of the baskets of daisies and Queen Anne's lace since they had been among the gatherers along with Ellen and the bridesmaids, and other village friends. The big day, a warm clear one, was here. The big moment had arrived.

Across the street on the Phillips' front porch, Uncle Ben and Aunt Dilsey watched first the surrey with its stately pace, and now the Eliza J. group. Dilsey noticed Miz Eliza was wearing real lady shoes and wondered if they hurt. The bridegroom had left some time ago with Mr. Charlie who was going to be the preacher at the wedding. It had been a long day, but Ben and Dilsey were pleased; they had helped by keeping Mr. Hedrick distracted with packing his bags, shining up his wedding shoes, and such like. That was one bustin'-to-go young man they'd known in his student days rushing in to eat at Miss Eliza's. The two were about to leave for the church themselves. Even though they were members there, they'd wait 'til the white folks were inside, then slip in the back.

Tense with conveying the bride, Oscar drove Prince at a molasses pace through the fragrant late afternoon. The surrey passed two slave cabins, crossed Pine, and passed the livery stable where a stable boy left off shaking a saddle blanket while the coach-of-state rolled by. He was put out that Oscar didn't even nod.

Over the tops of trees and buggies, Ellen could see the white steeple of the church. She knew the steeple was meant to point to heaven, but right now she felt it was pointing out to heaven what was about to take place within. She felt grateful to the Phillips and the Mitchells for pressing and collecting so that the town's Presbyterians had a church building. The white paint, a recent adornment, was still bright, and the squared columns seemed to greet her.

This was real. She, Ellen, was marrying and leaving her family and friends and Chapel Hill - leaving the South even. A swelling pushed at the sides of her throat. Organ music like a velvet ribbon was drawing her inside where Ben waited. She prayed in gratitude while also asking that she wouldn't cry.

Ben was waiting, trapped in the little room at the very back of the church behind the pulpit. He was closed in there with John Wheat and Professor Phillips who were guarding him closely to prevent any premature sighting of the bride. What was all this rigmarole for anyway? All he and Ellen wanted to do was to marry in the Lord's house and have His blessing on their life together. As far as he recalled, weddings had been a lot plainer back at the Pilgrim church of his childhood. He couldn't help thinking a lot of the goings-on were more to please the women involved than the Lord.

His throat was dry as sand. Perspiration ran down out of his hair into his beard so that he had to mop with his new handkerchief from the pocket of his new fawn-colored trousers. He glimpsed someone in a mirror and wondered who it was - the white-faced stranger with the slicked down dark hair and the good-looking frock coat.

"You could sit down, Ben," said Charles Phillips, amused at the restlessness of his old pupil. "I'll let you know when it's time."

"Never mind, Professor, this fellow is past help," John Wheat said.

Ben wondered why he'd asked John to be his best man anyway. Too bad Adam and the family couldn't be here. He noticed there was a view of the congregation through the slightly ajar door. He could see in slices by moving around. The church was packed so the flowers in the windows looked like continuations of ladies' bonnets. The world was in order; there sat Eliza J. herself, looking around to see if there was anything that needed straightening or polishing in the beribboned front pew where Pa would join her. Ben hoped he and Ellen would never lead such a separated marriage as those two did. The Thompson progeny sat behind them, except for Willie who would pump the organ.

Across from the Thompsons were the Phillips - Professor Charlie's parents and Sam and Laura. They were supposedly replacing the Hedricks. He wished for his own family but knew he and Ellen would go straight to the Davidson County on their wedding trip. He quickly checked the presence of Governor and Mrs. Swain who filled a pew with Anne, Eleanor and Richard. Thank the Lord there were some rows between the Mitchells and the Greens; trouble wasn't wanted. Present was just about the whole village and faculty, plus some Commencement visitors. He had a swift flash of realization that since the last Commencement he had become a part of a very different world.

He saw Dumps, Oscar, Aunt Dilsey and Uncle Ben standing behind the last pew like a dark honor guard. He felt they would rather have been invisible yet wanted to be present even at the cost being conspicuous. Still he realized he didn't really know the slaves' feelings. They were dressed-up and trying to take everything in. Harriet Beecher Stowe had probably never see their like-happy slaves. Things are really more relaxed here; we'll have to get used to the Yankee ways.

What was that? Yes, at last. The Lord's Prayer was being offered by the clear soprano voice of Mary Green. The three prisoners in the back room bowed their heads, knowing that when the prayer was over, they would be freed. Miss Ione caused the organ to wheeze forth the opening chords of the "Wedding March." Professor Phillips gestured for Ben and John to follow as his burly form entered the main room of the church. The three took their places facing the congregation, backed by an arbor of roses.

Called forth from the vestibule, the procession began. All eyes strained toward the back. Wearing boutonniere badges of office, groomsmen Shober, Richardson and Newcome advanced. Their expressions were sober, after all the tricks they'd threatened. Like good soldiers, they took their places to the left of the other men. Now everyone could watch the girls come in.

Here came Miss Corney, leading as always. Large and blue-gowned, she made her way briskly, nodding and smiling. Ben half-expected her to stop and make an announcement of some kind before she arrived at the front and turned. Mae Mitchell followed in a yellow gown, looking shyly down into her bouquet. Then came Sis Lina, quite lit up by the attention and her pink dress. Now all were in front of the roses which did smell delicious.

At last he could see her - Ellen, or a vision walking in a cloud, flowers crowning her veil. She held her father's arm, and her face was tilted so that Ben could not yet look into it. Hurry, hurry, he wanted to take her into his arms, and all this was in the way. Ill at ease, Pa Thompson made it real; he looked afraid she would break in two before he got her delivered. When the vision had floated to stand before the waiting court, Ben could see tears rolling down her cheeks. His own trembling stopped. When she finally looked into his eyes, he winked and offered his damp handkerchief.

When Pa Thompson had handed Ellen over to Ben and taken his seat beside his wife, Professor Phillips became the Reverend. His ruddy countenance very solemn he began the ritual in the book he had shown Ben earlier - the *Presbyterian Constitution*, printed in Philadelphia in 1841.

The proper silence followed his request that any impediment to this union be declared. Then he asked Ben and Ellen to join hand though they had already done so. He then "pronounced the marriage covenant" as the book instructed.

"Benjamin, you take this woman whom you hold by the hand, to be your lawful and married wife; and you promise and covenant, in the presence of God and these witnesses, that you will be unto her a loving and faithful husband, until you shall be separated by death."

As instructed, Ben responded, "I do." His heart was straining; this was either the end of everything or the beginning.

Ellen's cheeks were blooming and her eyes full of light. She answered her vows with a clear "Yes, I do," even though for her the word "obedient" was added to "loving and faithful." If asked to, she would have climbed the steeple.

Then it was quickly over. The Reverend Phillips pronounced them man and wife "according to the ordinance of God."

The crowded church relaxed in the heavy scent of roses, and, goal accomplished, Eliza sliced cake in her mind as Mary sang the closing blessing:

> Confirm it, God of love:
>
> Bless thy servants Deign this union to approve,
>
> and - on their head
>
> Now the oil of gladness shed;
>
> In this nuptial bond to thee
>
> Let them consecrated be.
>
> In prosperity be near,
>
> To preserve them in their fear;
>
> In affliction let thy smile
>
> All the woes of life beguile;
>
> And when every change is past,
>
> Take them to thy home at last.

It was a happy arrangement that neither the bridal couple nor the gathered company could foresee the afflictions and woes which would develop. For now, nothing marred the desperately anticipated happiness of this summer afternoon in the homey village.

Chapter Eleven

The long trip was by train from Raleigh, then by ship from Norfolk and past Mount Vernon on the Potomac. The anticipated return to this shrine was a little dimmed for Ben because the moon didn't cooperate but hid behind some clouds. Still, the ship's bells rang, men removed their hats, tribute was paid to the Father of the country.

Ellen was in that foreign land, The North. Unconsciously she was alert to adjust to whatever might conspire to throw a Southerner off balance. Mostly she was absorbed in trying to realize she was married-married and on a honeymoon. Already Ma and Sis Lina and Chapel Hill seemed another world of which she was no longer a part.

As the ship churned the waters of the Potomac, she watched her new husband with more interest than she found in the black hillside where Mount Vernon was reputed to be. He stood erect, facing the home of the hero.

"Isn't this wonderful, honey! Just think, General Washington lived up there!"

"Yes, I'm glad to be with you in the place that means so much to you. I remember you wrote to me about passing here on your trip up last year." She shivered, and his arm around her shoulders felt it.

"Ellen, are you cold? I could get your shawl from the cabin."

"No of course I'm not cold. It's so muggy I can hardly breathe. Must I say why I shivered?" She put her face close to his. "Can't you figure it out?" She felt the brush of his beard against her skin.

"Should I be able to? I'm not used to having a wife, you know. Women are a puzzle to me."

"With all those sisters you helped raise? I doubt that, Ben Hedrick. And besides, I'm not 'women,' I am your wife who loves you so much she shivers when you touch her, even when that fat man over there is trying to see what the honeymoon couple is doing."

"Ellen, you're teasing me! I'm surprised, not to mention pleased." He moved his arm to encircle her waist and spread his fingers so that the tips just touched the rise of her bosom.

"Ben!" She was embarrassed.

"Wait, I'll do that again, our friend is looking away."

She smiled and he could see her white teeth and showed her his in return. She took his hand, and Mr. and Mrs. Hedrick retired to their cabin for the night. Mount Vernon was miles behind.

They took a coach for Cambridge from Boston, a city Ellen decided she liked. It was a big city but not so overwhelming as New York.

"We'll visit a lot of the old places," Ben promised. It was such a pleasure having the company of his sweet little wife who was an even greener traveler than himself. He anticipated taking her to Faneuil Hall and the Old North Church and to hearthe famous abolitionist William Lloyd Garrison for a real blood-warmer. It would be even better to be here in the bustling North with a companion who shared his outlook, Ben told her.

"There's Harvard College," he pointed out as they passed tall brick columns and a graceful iron gate. "Not much like the little stone walls at our dear old Carolina college, but then it's lots older - 1638 compared to our 1792."

"1638! Ben, how could it be that old? The United States isn't that old!"

"That's right, sweetheart, Harvard was set up in the early days of the colony. Thoroughly British, you know, Madam."

The driver called out from his seat above them, "Here you are, sir, Brattle House." Called out before he's even stopped the horses, Ellen noticed. Ben didn't seem to take heed, she realized he was used to the fast ways of Yankees and their rush to get on to the next customer.

She saw a large three-story brick building which made Picard's in Chapel Hill look like a cabin. Ben took her arm and helped her down from the coach. She was standing on a street made of brick pavers beside a white picket fence. The driver carried their two small trunks, at Ben's direction, and followed them as they began their life at Brattle House on Brattle Street in Cambridge.

"Mrs. Wentworth," Ben called as he ushered Ellen into the lobby.

"Oh, there you are, Mr. Hedrick - and your new wife!" The proprietor's voice was sharp but she had a face that smiled like a pale ginger cookie with a raisin grin. Ellen stepped forward to be hugged, forgetting Ben had warned her that Yankees weren't much on showing affection. Poor things, she thought as she shook the proprietor's hand. He'd told her too how lucky they were to have a room at Brattle House, a popular place close to the campus and to his office. It even had a ballroom.

Ellen gave Mrs. Wentworth her best smile. "How do you do, Mrs. Wentworth. I'm so glad you can take us in."

"I'm glad too, Mrs. Hedrick," she said, her sharp way of pronouncing words making Ellen feel her own speech dripped Southern honey. That's my way of talking, she thought, and I'm not changing it. Still, she felt comfortable with plump, corseted Mrs. Wentworth in her white embroidered apron. Not much like with Ma in her flour-sacking one.

"Come along, you'll be wanting to get settled before dinner, I'm sure," Mrs. Wentworth said as she led the way up the narrow and rather dark stairway. The house had a more closed-in feeling than Ma's but also felt more stout.

"Here's your room, a corner front. You're fortunate the Brownlees just moved out, and Mr. Hedrick had it reserved before he left last month. My rooms don't stay vacant, you know," she added in the most matter-of-fact way. "You'll hear the dinner gong at six," she said over her shoulder as she turned to go, not waiting to see how Ellen liked the room.

When the driver had placed the trunks on the window seat at Ben's direction, received his tip, and closed the door behind him, Ellen sat down in the high-backed rocker and closed her eyes.

Ben turned from checking their outside view.

"What's the matter, love, don't you like it?"

She opened her eyes and smiled at him. "I think it's the nicest room in the world, and my husband is a clever man to get it for us. I'm just a little weary from traveling, I reckon."

He felt a protective rush for this more delicate person who was now a part of himself. "Of course you are. But when you feel like it, look out here. If you lean out just a little, you can see the river. Used to be a clear view before all those buildings went up. This street, Brattle, was where all the rich folks lived before the Revolution. They had to clear out from Tory Row, as it was called, when the Patriots took over this area in earnest." He stopped to test whether Ellen was asleep behind those closed eyes.

She murmured something about how he could know so much and smiled without opening her eyes. Her husband watching her was a contented man.

October 1852

There wasn't another place Ellen would rather be. Cambridge in October was entirely satisfactory. Mornings she puttered around their room, playing the lady - seeing to their clothes, arranging her hair in the pouf she saw on the young ladies of Cambridge and Boston, chatting with Nora the chambermaid. She made a game of whether Ben, with his head full of the trajectories of planets, would notice a new hairdo or an arrangement of asters on the dresser. And she read.

Such an abundance to read, and, for the first time, she had the leisure with no housework, child care or table-setting to do. This leisure would end next May, she knew. After her daily *Bible* reading, she read *Harper's Illustrated*, the *North American Review*, *The Liberator*, and volumes of Longfellow, their neighbor further up Brattle Street.

One day Mrs. Wentworth came in for a visit before dinnertime. She told Ellen that the famous Margaret Fuller, whose Memoirs Ben had sent last winter, had lived on their street in the old house with the marker, "House of William Brattle, 1727."

Ellen suspected Mrs. Wentworth of enjoying gossip much like some of the Chapel Hill women. She told Ellen that Margaret was peculiar, being so brilliant and all, but not a woman you'd forget. And she was truly sorry Margaret had died at sea with her new Italian husband and their baby. Sad really. "But who can say," she went on to say, "Whether God was punishing that woman? They say the baby was born before they were married, you know. That sort of thing is hardly civilized and certainly not Christian, not that Margaret ever pretended to be that. But she was a good writer, a regular newspaper correspondent, you know."

Ellen had learned that Mrs. Wentworth was a faithful Episcopalian who prided herself on being broad-minded. Her questions to Ellen about what it was like to live with slaves allowed her position on slavery to show plainly. She planned to draw Mrs. Wentworth out further while assuring her that her family's servants didn't have all that hard a life. She knew you had to choose your words carefully on the topic, and she wanted to learn more about the thinking of people up here.

"Yes, it is remarkable," the older woman continued, "the interesting lives that have been lived on this old street." Growing up in Concord, she couldn't say she ever felt close to Margaret Fuller but a lot of Cambridge and Boston women hung around her and her preaching of women's rights. She was part of that Emerson/Thoreau crowd, Brook Farm and all that and Mrs. W. couldn't say just what they were all up to, but it's a free country, she assured Ellen. Anyway, she knew for sure that when Margaret Fuller had lived on Brattle Street, she'd gone out to work every day, just like a man. Speak not ill of the dead, she always said.

Ellen mulled such voluminous additions to her storehouse of knowledge. But she was never so absorbed, curled up in a rocker by the window, as to forget the approach of one o'clock. Ben would be leaving the *Almanac* and walking home to dinner which was served promptly at one. He was usually dashing into the dining room just as serving began. Ellen suspected Mrs. W. of delaying a few minutes for the benefit of her favorite, Mr. Hedrick.

And so they would eat their codfish stew or boiled beef and potatoes followed by Indian pudding "in all its blandness" as Ben said upstairs. Brattle House fare was certainly not the equal of Ma's. Why, Ellen hadn't had a hot biscuit or any good country ham since being in Cambridge. But then there wasn't any Little Dumps back in the kitchen. Instead there was Mrs. Ryan whose Irish cuisine was fighting it out toe-to-toe with Mrs. Wentworth's New England one. Ellen and Ben had a lot of fun out of the contest and kept score privately.

Afternoons were what they lived for. Ben was postponing his courses at the Lawrence Scientific School of the University for the first semester - just one reason Ellen wrote to her friend Julie: "Mr. H. deserves all you think of him. Of his sterner virtues I was aware but did not know a head so strong owned a heart so deep and true." Faithfully in the afternoons, Ben took her out to explore the world of Harvard, Cambridge, and Boston.

A walk of just a few blocks took them into the golden world of the Harvard yard in autumn. The great old elms and the ruddy weathered brick buildings combined to make an enchanting scene. Ellen had to fight feelings of disloyalty if she compared this to her hometown university, also a beauty of trees and old buildings. Harvard was a very special place, she could tell. She could see Learning written all over it. Learning and Tradition. There was just so much more of it. It was deeper, taller and wider than dear old Chapel Hill.

It was all enclosed with iron fences and brick posts and entered through that graceful gateway which would be the envy of Governor Swain. The Governor would probably also like to appropriate Harvard Hall with its beautiful bell tower. Ben said a man who became the governor's enemy and a Revolutionary hero built the tower for a royal governor - in 1764 -. Most everything here had to do with Revolutionary times, Ellen felt. Or maybe her escort's interest in that period made him emphasize it when showing her around.

They walked hand-in-hand through Harvard Yard in a rain of gold leaves. One of the gray-haired professors tipped his hat as they met. Ben tipped his, Ellen nodded her green satin bonnet and smiled her demure yet open smile. As the couple passed, the older man stood looking after them; they were the picture of happiness and confidence, or his name wasn't Jared Sparks. He hoped the university he headed would meet their needs, whatever they were.

As they walked on, Ben whispered an explanation of who that man was. Jared Sparks, the president of Harvard, had single-handedly saved most of the letters of the early patriots to be treasured by future generations.

One day, as soon as Ben was free, they took the horse-cars into the city. He told her, "We're going to have dinner at the oldest eating place in Boston, but don't worry, sugarfoot, the food is fresh."

"Ben Hedrick, if I wasn't hungry, I might laugh."

"Never mind. It's Union Oyster House, Daniel Webster's favorite."

"Well, that's not such a good thing, he died last week, remember?" When seated in the busy restaurant, they decided on a lobster dinner and enjoyed it with gusto.

Ellen was happy to have her own tour guide in such a richly historic city. "Now Ben, when are we going to see Faneuil Hall?" she wanted to know as they emerged from the Oyster House.

"In time, in time, dear. Let's just stroll along and drink in the history."

"I'll try, Ben, but I'm awfully full of lobster."

"All right. Ellen, meet Samuel Adams," he said, turning her to face a statue on a pedestal by the street.

"How do you do, Mr. Adams? Excuse me, but I don't really know who you are. John Adams, I know, and John Quincy Adams. Where do you fit in?"

Ben stood on the base of Sam's pedestal and answered, "Why, Miss, how does it happen you don't know the famous leader of the patriot underground? I was part of the Boston Massacre. I entertained at the Boston Tea Party. Even if you are a Southerner, madam - as I can tell by your accent - you should recall my name as a signer of the momentous Declaration of Independence."

Ellen bowed slightly. "Please excuse me, Mr. Adams. It just slipped my mind but I'll always remember you now."

"See that you do, madam," the statue continued. "Ahem, those other fellows, they were my second cousins, I reckon."

Ellen laughed, and her bonnet feathers danced. "Oh, Ben, Mr. Adams never said 'I reckon' in his life. I've noticed that must be a strictly Southern expression."

He stepped down, and the small crowd that had begun to gather, dispersed, the statue had gone silent again. "Now for Faneuil Hall, the famous," he said, taking her arm and turning her about. "Behold the Cradle of Liberty."

"Oh, Ben, it's right here - and it's so small."

"Think so? It's seen many an important meeting. I was here last July and heard the reading of the Declaration. They read it every year to honor those good ol' fellows pledging to fight for freedom with their lives, their fortunes and their sacred honor."

They stood carefully studying the old three-story building, trying to overhear history.

"Bet you don't know the first woman to speak in Faneuil," Ellen challenged her husband.

"No, but I'd guess one of the abolitionists. Was it Harriet Beecher Stowe?"

Ellen smiled to have caught him. "No, believe it or not, it was a Southern woman. She and her husband are abolitionist leaders, though. I read about her in Mr. Garrison's paper. She's Angelina Grimke, and she was from Charleston."

"Was is right. I expect she was from some other place from then on."

"I think she'd already been banished because she wrote an abolitionist pamphlet aimed at Southern women."

Ben squeezed her arm and she knew he was proud of her.

Sunday, October 30

After dinner, Ben sat down to reply to Charles Phillip's letter. He and Ellen had gone to hear the famous Congregationalist preacher Theodore Parker at the Music Hall in the morning. As usual there was a huge crowd to hear what Ben considered a simplistic sermon. Parker's insistence on the immorality of slavery was hard to refute, however. It rang in Ben's mind, stirring deep echoes of Grandfather

Sherwood and his moving away because of slavery.

Now there was time to organize his response to Professor Phillip's stunning proposition, which certainly must have Governor Swain's approval.

My dear Sir:

I received yours of the 21st Oct. and it was very timely. I was so undecided about my future that I was beginning to be ashamed of myself. And though this holds out very uncertain prospects, I was pleased without knowing exactly why. For a young man without any experience in teaching to go to NC and expect to make a living from the pupils he can attract, seems to border on the visionary. But if I have the encouragement of the faculty and a few others, I shall be willing to try and hope to succeed.

The establishment of a scientific school of some kind at Chapel Hill, I think is a very good idea. It has been a cherished plan with me for some time. As the courses you offer now did not leap like Minerva into existence, it is not probable that a Scientific School would do. But if it were properly commenced, I have little doubt it would soon gain respect among similar institutions in other parts of the country.

The college possessed the element of growth ever since its foundation, whereas the state as a whole is said to be going backwards while standing still. It is not very pleasant, as I have several times experienced, to meet a Yankee and find he knows North Carolina only as a turpentine producer.

But backwardness is not the case in everything about N.C. The jurists and statesmen who have received their early training at the University have always ranked second to none in the country. North Carolina has yet to know the total of her own resources and is known still less by others.

I look forward to hearing more about the still undigested plan for the new School.

Your first letter has remained unanswered so long that you may have thought I'd forgotten it. To convince you that I have not, I will answer in part your question, "What are you doing?" You wish to know what I am doing. You should not question too closely a newly married man. I thought I had the right to relax for a few months whenever the immediate duties of my office permitted. So I will account to you only for office work.

The moon-culmination of part of the year for the

Almanac occupied me the first month of my return. Since then I have assisted in correcting OH, getting through the press the balance which will soon be published, and the rest of the time preparing Mr. Bond's new method of perturbation, with an example. Next week, with Mr. Kerr to help me, I expect to commence the ephemeris of the moon for 1856. We have a new set of lunar table prepared by the office. The printing of them in a beautiful quarto volume is nearly finished; they will shortly be published to the world.

Then, recalling his old teacher's interest in the mathematics class of Professor Pierce, Ben set down a page of theorems, transformations of coordinates, curves and functionaries. He could picture the red face of Professor Phillips leaning over the page with such pleasure that his turned-down lips threatened to turn up. He wouldn't be easy to work with.

Chapter Twelve

**Brattle House
January 1853**

Yesterday Ben wrote Governor Swain of the momentous decision they had come to. He would become Professor Hedrick of the University, rather than of Davidson College which had also made him an offer. He and Ellen would return to Chapel Hill but not until January of 1854. The deciding had been a welcome distraction from the near-complete absorption in the growth of the expected baby.

Ellen prodded the coal fire in the grate as she prepared to finish dressing for the day. The tray Ben had brought up for her from the dining room sat with its empty dishes on top of the chest near the door. What a darling he was to be so considerate of her. Since she became pregnant he'd been even more solicitous than before. Smoothing down the side of her dark plaid dress, she smiled at the sizable bulge developing at her waist. Thank you, Lord. It was so right that their love should have fruit. Please let it be a healthy infant.

She hadn't been subject to the morning sickness she had considered inevitable from all the talk in Chapel Hill parlors. But then, Ma, always exceptional, hadn't been queasy either.

A polite knock on the door probably meant Mrs. Murrett. Yes.

She had a kind face set in the ruffles of her cap like a bonbon or an iced almond.

"Good morning, my dear," Mrs. Murrett said in her clear but gentle New York accent. Her eyes went to Ellen's waistline.

This was the day Ellen would enlighten the older woman about her expectations. "Come in, Mrs. Murrett. I'm getting so lazy since Ben brings up my breakfast that I've just this minute gotten into my clothes. Sit here by the fire while I give my hair a lick or two."

Long rhythmic strokes of the brush were the warp of their conversation. Copper lights worked through the tawny softness.

"Yes, we've missed you in the dining room. Mr. Hedrick is extremely thoughtful of you, my dear Mrs. Hedrick."

"Yes, he is, and you've probably guessed he has a particular reason just now. If you haven't, I'll tell you, but I'd rather you didn't tell anyone else, at least for awhile..."

The two women smiled at each other, another moment of the ages-long conspiracy. It is for woman to know what life really is. Men can only do their part and stand by.

Mrs. Murrett said nothing out of deference to the little bride who was going through such an exciting time of her life. It was Ellen's time to speak if she chose. Alice Murrett had had her day, and her grown children were having theirs.

Ellen stopped brushing and sat still, her long shining hair framing her radiant face. "Yes, I'm expecting a little one! Isn't it wonderful!"

"Of course it's wonderful, Ellen." Mrs. Murrett slowly rose from her chair and went to embrace Ellen where she sat. "You and Mr. Hedrick will make very fine parents, I'm sure," she said resuming her seat and readjusting the black shawl around her shoulders. "When do you expect this big event to take place?"

"Probably late April or early May. We are delighted, of course. Mrs. Murrett, I'm so glad you're here with me." Her eyes filled, though she still smiled.

"You know I want to be your friend, Ellen. Maybe even something of a mother since you're so far from home. We'll see it through together."

"Oh, thank you for understanding, Mrs. Murrettt. You see, I'm from a small town, knowing everybody, and my stepmother running the family. In a way I'm glad we have this chance to be on our own up North and to get off on a good start in our marriage. Can't tell but what Ma and Ben would cross swords over something or other. Both have decided opinions, you see."

"Of course. God is good to you. You have to build your own home. Your Ma would agree to that even though she might work hard to make it hard for you - not that she would mean to."

"Now how in the world did you know that?"

"Just from what I've observed about Mr. Hedrick and what you've said about Mrs. Thompson and read from her letters. They do have decided opinions, but I'm convinced they both really care about you."

"I know they do, and I'm grateful to the Lord." Ellen stood and faced the mirror. She began to lift her hair and pin it up. "I'm glad I told you."

"I'm glad too, my dear Ellen. It's the most natural thing in the world. Please just say so if there's anything at all I can help with - not that I have any kind of authority except the kind you get from experience." She rose with a rustle of her skirt.

"That's just what I need," Ellen said, opening the door for her good friend.

The noon booming of the grandfather clock on the landing shocked her from the trance in which she sat holding the *North Carolina Standard* of January 19, 1853. She decided to reread what had hypnotized her. Mr. Holden had reprinted a long and unbelievable review of Uncle Tom's Cabin from the *British Army Dispatch*. Ellen understood that British textile firms were anxious to stay on good terms with the American South in the tension about slavery. She would ask Ben if that was the explanation for this thing.

The reviewer was certainly original to begin by saying he hadn't read the book. But that did not prevent him from believing it to be "devoid of truth, principle, and reality." Then he really slandered poor Harriet. "We can imagine her endowed with an awful sense of womanhood, and to make - if she ever considered such a task since the second edition of her book was sold - about the worst dumplings that were ever placed on dingy tablecloth in a slovenly place. We can imagine that she writes with a big slovenly hand, the letters all backwards, avoiding neatness with painstaking precision - her voice is probably harsh, her attitude imposing, and she wears her own gray hair in the mothers-of-nations style. Still we think it a great pity that she did not do anything but what she has done, with all the busy enthusiasm of a woman in britches."

Well, Ellen thought, I am certainly going to get that book everyone is talking about and read it. Maybe I could even go to the famous Miss Peabody's bookstore and buy it. She felt angry for the renowned Mrs. Stowe and proud that a woman had written such an exciting book.

Late February

The Yankee winter had not begun to relax its grip, though February was almost over. The Hedricks sat in their Queen Anne chairs in the cozy room at Brattle House while the fire simmered in the grate and the oil lamps shone brightly. Ellen worked on her endless succession of tiny garments; this evening found her feather stitching the hem of a small flannel gown. Its future occupant seemed to kick at the creamy material from its citadel within.

Ben was reading the latest *Standard*, which had arrived that day from Raleigh. "Honestly, Ellen, I don't know why we subscribe to King Billy's rag!"

She smiled at the outraged tone, which had become his ritual reaction to Holden's paper. "What's got you upset with Billy now? I think it's something of a bargain. Why it's cheaper than spring tonic and cleans the blood better - heats it to a boiling point."

He gave her a grin but went on with an angry tone. "Just listen to this. It's headed "The Slavery Question." 'Do not be shocked, good reader, by the heading of this article - it is not our intention to go into a discussion of the Slavery question. We have had enough of that. It is true we should not fear such a discussion, for we regard African slavery as established on the impregnable foundation of Holy Scripture, but then we can perceive no necessity AT THIS TIME for arguments in defence of the institution. Our purpose is to call attention to the evil - if we may use so strong a word - which people of the South are, to no small extent, bringing on themselves by continuing this very discussion.'"

Ben crunched the newspaper in his hand and puffed the steam from his cheeks. "Can you believe it, Ellen? He's all for keeping the door shut on free speech. He makes me so mad!" His blue eyes shot sparks. "But wait, there's more."

"'Mr. Paige of Winchester, Virginia, is publishing soon a work entitled "Uncle Robin in his cabin in Virginia and Tom without one in Boston." Not strictly a reply to Uncle Tom says the *Alexander Gazette* but it presents a just and dispassionate aspect of the subject so partially and unfairly presented by Mrs. Stowe.'"

"Well, Ben, we agreed Mrs. Stowe's book was overdrawn."

"Yes, in our experience, but we also agreed her view is shared by lots of folks - look at our friends up here in Cambridge and how many are convinced of the immorality of slavery. Just like Grandfather and the Quakers back in North Carolina. They base their views on the Bible a lot more soundly than Billy Holden and his Lords of the Lash backers."

Ellen made another stitch in blue on Piggy's gown. They had agreed to call the little unseen member Piggy since the name served for either sex and since the way he was growing predicted a good feeder.

"Ellen, just let me finish reading you this amazing tripe."

"I didn't say anything, Ben. I'm listening."

"You're patient with me, dear girl. All right... 'Mrs. Stowe's book is that of a prejudiced and depraved mind.' Then, hmmm, the old boy says some ask what good Paige's book can do. 'Fanatics won't be convinced. What they want is discussion which is another name for agitation.'

"I tell you, Ellen, things are closing down in the Old North State."

"I think you're right. I guess being up here we can take a wider view, don't you think? Go ahead, what else does the planters' mouthpiece say?"

He read, "'Southern people ask to be let alone. They don't intend to abandon this institution despite all opposition because they accept it as God's will.'"

"He goes on, 'Shall we be silent when works similar to Mrs. Stowe's appear? Yes, be silent and let your deeds speak for you. Be silent rather than reply to such people and such attacks...what the latter class (the ignorant and depraved) want is a contest over slavery, and by meeting such people halfway we give them that contest.'"

The room was silent except for the stewing of the fire.

"It just doesn't seem right to me, Ellen. You can see I'm bothered. Reminds me of the first time I met Governor Swain and he warned me that slavery was not to be discussed. But this nation was founded on freedom - of people, of ideas, of speech, of press."

"Of course, you know I feel the same way. It hurts to see our home state in such a trap and our families and friends in it too. And ourselves, too, Ben, unless things change before we go back." She folded her needlework, and looked at him. Their eyes spoke reassurance to each other. "Thank God I'm free to love you, my darling," she said, rescued from worry.

He rose and went to her, knelt and put his head in her lap. They were both aware of the little shape pushing from her, touching Ben's dark head, and their laughter blended.

Ben said, "Piggy says, 'I'm glad too.'"

April 1853

As she grew rounder and riper with new life, Ellen felt in harmony with the welcome burst of spring in the world outside the room at Brattle House. One April morning she sat down to write a long overdue letter to Polly Paisley Rankin, a mentor back in Edgeworth days and wife of Ben's prized teacher back in the country. She wrote freely knowing she would correct and copy the letter to one who still inspired awe. After greetings she wrote:

> We are both happy as can be. Ben is more studious than he was at first, busily preparing himself for his new duties from nine in the morning 'til dark, excepting an hour for dinner. He is at his office, attending lectures, or experimenting in the laboratory. He is very fond of his chemical studies, so finds but little time for literature.
>
> My time has been devoted much to French, have read several Moliere comedies. Think I do very well. There are

so many old standard works for me to read that I do not have as much time to devote to new books, as I would like.

We have two bookstores quite near where we can see anything we wish. We ought perhaps to make better use of them than we do, we cannot hope to have the same advantage again, at least for many years.

Have not read any of the replies to Mrs. Stowe except Aunt Phillis - and that is so poor it does not deserve the name. I think there is too much truth in what Mrs. Stowe says for it to be refuted. I know no Legrees myself but think it would not be hard to find many of his first cousins, if not brothers, in the Eastern part of our own Carolina. Novel writers and newspaper editors would do much better to tell us some way to lessen the evil than to try to make folks believe there is no evil in it. They will be trying to make us believe darkness a greater blessing than light the next thing we know.

The winter, everybody says, was unusually mild. Only two snows deep enough for sleighing. Then we had lovely times. In the morning or the evening I could stand at my window and see the sleighs. As soon as one was out of my sight, another was in it. The bells made merry. The nights *were moonlit. Sometimes it would be twelve o'clock before the sleighing ended. The coldest weather was mid-March when the thermometer stood at 8 above zero for several days. Since then we have had the most delightful weather. The buds are swelling, some maples are in bloom. I saw a few crocuses blooming today, the first of the season for me.*

Then she added a note to the paragraph on Mrs. Stowe's book. "If we feel that slavery is wrong, some of the congressmen, including Mr. Venable, acknowledge we had better admit it rather than attempt to hide from its fruits."

Ben and Ellen had begun to wrestle with the morality of slavery, an issue that would affect the rest of their lives.

Then she pampered herself by putting away her rough draft and postponing the rewriting until tomorrow. She realized she had said nothing about her real preoccupation, the impending birth, but she hadn't planned to tell Mrs. Rankin. Time enough after the baby was in her arms.

Chapter Thirteen

Cambridge
May-August 1853

It was Eliza J. who masterminded the arrival of Selina Morrow near the time of Ellen's delivery. It was neither Ben nor Ellen who had suggested the visit although both were pleased that the well-loved Sis Lina was actually there in Cambridge.

Everyone agreed that it was of mutual benefit. The Hedricks were delighted to have the familiar narrow face and generous presence there for the birth of their first child. And Selina herself was highly pleased to have such a good reason to travel - and to travel a long way at that. It was a treat for her. She'd never made a real trip, not even to Virginia.

So here she was in Boston, well, almost Boston, actually Cambridge, which Ellen had written about and Benjamin too before he was Ellen's husband. It was another world, even further from Chapel Hill than the distance in miles - so much thicker with people - she'd never get used to it. The horse-cars, the drays, the huddled buildings! She was comforted by the realization that she'd never have to get used to it. Ellen had Ben to steady her up here, and Selina wasn't jealous of that handsome and brilliant man. She herself was certain to have a husband someday but it wouldn't be one that would force her to live up North. You could never be sure but that you're talking to an abolitionist.

She hadn't let on how frightened she was riding the train. The noise and the shaking were almost beyond bearing at first, but she figured she'd better get used to it since she had to stay on it a long time to get to Ellen in her hour of need and also to get back home to Raleigh and Chapel Hill again- and Henry. Being away made her lonesome for Henry, but she didn't let on to Ellen.

The main thing Selina wondered about all the people riding the trains and filling up the cities was: where on earth were they all going? She reckoned they all knew who they were and that they had families at home, but the possibility seemed remote. Why you could fit Chapel Hill into one corner of the park, or Commons, as they called it in Boston. And the way they talked! It was all she could do to take it in; she developed the habit of putting her hand on the arm of the speaker and asking sweetly, "Would you mind saying that again?"

But her real goal was getting to Ellen, and somehow she was eventually there settled into a room down the hall from Ellen and Ben at the elegant Brattle House. Would this place make Ma's eyes stare! The student and professor boarders on Franklin Street seemed small potatoes compared to Harvard and Cambridge.

She'd seen some pretty sights too - flowering spring trees and bright jonquils such as were long finished blooming at home. But you had to look sharp to see natural things in the middle of all these people coming together so close. "Clare, it makes me feel right smothery," she confided to Ellen, not wanting Mrs. Murrett or the others to overhear for fear they'd think her a country bumpkin.

'Course seeing Ellen so round and about to pop scared her a little. She was used to Ma as an expectant mother, but this didn't seem like the same thing at all. Ma was tall and broad and seemed like she was just carrying a package under her apron. But Ellen was small and short and looked like a little mule pushing a big load- actually like the package was carrying her. Selina was a little unnerved but tried to hide it laughing and joking with Ellen during the days when Ben was away. She even felt a little edgy toward Mr. Hedrick for doing this to Ellen though she knew that didn't make sense ~ Ellen loving him so much.

That was what mattered, Selina figured, the love of a man and woman. There was a man for Selina somewhere (not up here, though). It was romantic even if poor Ellen had all she could do to move around. Lucky for Northern ladies, they could just walk into a dining room like here at Brattle House and get their meals (such as they were). They didn't have to cook for themselves and their families. Selina's many years of helping in Ma's boardinghouse made this seem the height of luxury. Didn't seem fair. Why should Yankee women have it so easy? And some of them were writing and marching about women's rights!

She liked her room with its pretty woven bedspread, polished washstand and its decorated bowl and pitcher. And she liked having the maid bring coal for the fireplace on cool mornings. She liked the maid too, though she was harder to understand than Mrs. Murrett and the others at their table. Said she was from Ireland and hadn't been in America but five months. Maureen was her name. Said she was glad Missus Morrow had come to see her sister "the fair bairn nigh to giving birth to her babe."

As April wore on and May began, Selina began to get anxious. Why didn't the baby come?

At last, early in the morning on the third day of May, Ben tapped on her door and said, "Selina, it's time. Could you come and stay with Ellen while I go for Dr. Reed?"

She jumped into a wrapper and out her door into theirs. Ellen was lying there in the high bed, perspiration threading down her face. She put out her hand and said, smiling, "Oh, Sis Lina, Piggy is on the way! Stay with me, won't you?"

For this she had come a thousand miles. Ellen's hand grasped her sister's and never let go until Ben came in with the puffing doctor - which was after she had a series of spasms coming closer and closer together. It was hard to know which girl was more relieved when the two men came into the room.

Hours were to pass before the newborn's cry changed the tension in the front corner room to joy. The mother's tears ran down smiling cheeks. When Selina had called Ben from the hallway, he came, put his head down beside Ellen and sobbed with relief. The little red man-child was handed to his Aunt Selina who bathed him, wrapped him snugly, and placed him in his mother's arms.

Ellen was not prepared for the exaltation of looking into eyes opening and seeing for the first time. Wordsworth's words, "trailing clouds of glory do we come" came to her as she saw radiance in her baby's little countenance.

His grandfather's names had already been chosen, should a boy be born. He would be "John" for John Leonard Hedrick down in Davidson County and "Thompson" for William Thompson of Rock Spring, Orange County, But for now he was still Piggy.

Selina stayed to help with the baby until Ellen felt well set on her new course. Sometimes feeling in the way of the little family, she took walks around Cambridge and even ventured into Boston.

One afternoon Mrs. Murrett's daughter Ruth went with her. Disaster! While having tea downstairs on their return, the two fell out over the subject of slavery, *Uncle Tom's Cabin* being the opening salvo. Ruth asked Selina if she found the book to present a true picture of the life of slaves in the South, and the southern girl choked on her shortbread. Ruth was amazed when her small talk triggered such a red-faced response but it was too late. Selina finally stammered, "Certainly not!" but was too conflicted to substantiate her outrage. They returned upstairs in silence and continued ignorance of the other's point of view.

That summer, Ben's mentor, Professor Charles Phillips, came up to study at Harvard, and he spent time with the Hedricks and their guest. He was studying drawing related to the civil engineering courses he would teach in the new department at UNC, which would also include Ben's chemistry courses.

Ellen was glad to have her friend Corney's brother around, although she found him a little intimidating. Ben tried to share some of his own course-planning with the older man. The Professor's blustery presence wasn't as constant as Selina's adaptable one, but he was a part of their lives when his work gave him leisure - and when he wasn't writing home.

The Hedricks would have been amazed at what their friend wrote to his wife in regard to how life in the North was influencing him, Ben. Phillips' view was prophetic in foreseeing future trouble from their having absorbed a different perspective on such a volatile issue as slavery. His provincialism on Darwinism would have surprised them less. His concern for Ben's spiritual life relates to their all being members of the Chapel Hill Presbyterian Church.

On August 22, a short while before he was to return home escorting Selina Morrow, Charles Phillips wrote:

> My dearest wife,
>
> I have just received your letter from home. They laugh at me for being homesick but I stoutly deny the charge. But to tell you the truth, I would be mighty glad to be with you all.
>
> Mr. Hedrick and I went to hear Dr.Beecher yesterday morning - "The fool hath said in his heart"...an excellent practical talk on human depravity. The doctor draws his picture with a heavy hand and a soft crayon, there's no mistaking his object. I like to hear old, experienced and lively preachers. They talk right at one with a voice of authority.
>
> Mr. Hedrick was vexed by the old man's certitude. "Why, he says, he never allowed there was ever any other possible view of human nature, and his distinctions were not numerous nor nice enough." You know that I have expressed fears that Hedrick's running about to hear celebrities had led him away from the simplicity of our Faith as it is in Jesus. I really fear greatly for him. He has got some abominable notions in his head, such as

amelioration of mankind: every effort that proceeds, fails, and is succeeded by another and better one. I was truly surprised to hear him thus retail Parkerism.

I must go over and show him the evil tendency of such speculations. Just think of his coming with a bright face to illustrate the coincidence of God's predestination and man's free agency by some recondite property of a curved line and the algebraic process by which we find its peculiarities.

I told him such things were truly trifling and dangerous. Thereat he seemed to be silenced for a while. But you must not talk about these things or folks will spread it that Hedrick is an infidel. Our folks do not understand the speculative atmosphere men of thought inhabit here, and any crossing-over of long-preserved lines is to them, profane. Truly it is dangerous, but I must allow it also to be enticing. With another I might look at some of these queer views, but not with him...

How often I think of you and pray for you that we may serve our generation faithfully and that you may be kept safe under the Almighty's wings.

Yours affectionately,

Charles Phillips

At the end of August, Ben and Ellen and little John were alone as the Chapel Hill outpost in Cambridge. Selina was at home telling traveler's tales and quelling an occasional whispered question about Benjamin's orthodoxy. Charles Phillips was back wearing his professor hat, pushing aside his own questions about Hedrick's vulnerability to Northern influence. The Hendricks' return was anticipated before the New Year.

Chapter Fourteen

Chapel Hill
January-March 1854

"My dear, you look as bright as a summer day!" Governor Swain beamed down on Ellen as snowflakes began to fall on Franklin Street.

"Thank you, Governor Swain," she answered. "Say hello to Pig -uh, Johnnie." She turned to the well-wrapped bundle that was her son in the arms of Melie.

"Evening, Melie," the big man greeted the little nursemaid.

Melie made her manners with a smile and a duck of her head. She held Johnnie up for the Governor to see but declined to pull the cover from his head. You had to take care a baby didn't get snow on him; it was bad for their heads.

"Hello, Johnnie," Swain said, bending down to look into the little face, already familiar since his mother had brought him to visit before Christmas. "Ellen, he's a lucky boy, looks like his mother instead of his father."

Ellen couldn't think of how to respond to that utter falsehood.

He continued, "'Course, if he's got the brain of his father, he's a mighty fortunate young man. Mighty fortunate." He was thinking you have to walk on eggs talking to a mother about her child.

"I agree with you there, sir," Ellen said, thinking he got out of that gaffe handily. "How is Mrs. Swain today?" she continued.

"She's very well, considering her nerves and what she has to put up with - the children shut in and full of vinegar. I'm going to the store now to get her some of that nerve medicine she thinks is a help."

Ellen thought it was the Swain children that needed a tonic, a tonic called discipline, but she wouldn't have dreamed of saying so. "Well, come by to see us, Governor. Benjamin should be here by Saturday with that laboratory equipment. He's real anxious to get it set up."

The tall man continued to bend toward her as they talked. "And the University is just as eager for him to settle his *lares and penates*." And, he added internally, no one is more anxious than the President who went out on a limb with Charlie Phillips to start this thing. "Hope that letter is in the post office for you - and that you can read it," he called over his shoulder as they parted.

She smiled at his reference to Ben's atrocious handwriting. You don't hope it as much as I do, she thought. Her spirit rushed forward toward the final block down Franklin, only her body proceeded on course, with Melie and Johnnie in her wake. Her heart was full as she moved along the way of which she knew every stone and rut. Over there across the street where the campus lay ringed with trees, things had changed a little and all for the better. The walks and shrubs the English gardener had created made it more tame and more beautiful, she had to admit. She loved the scene especially having been away from it for so long. She was sorry to see pigs rooting in the newly planted rose arbor. Didn't seem fitting for a university with over 300 students to have roving pigs.

"Ellen Thompson, are you out of your mind!" It was Eliza J., a black shawl over her head, long apron over her dress. "What do you mean bringing that precious baby out in the snow?"

The big woman sounded angry, but Ellen knew she was just showing how much she cared for Johnnie.

"Oh, hello, Ma. Don't worry, Johnnie's used to being out in the snow you know, from Cambridge. The doctor up there said fresh air is good for babies, even if it's cold."

"Well, I tell you that sounds like a Yankee! Good for a baby! Don't you and Mr. Hedrick want to change your minds and move in with me? Then I could see to it Johnnie was prop'ly taken care of." She sniffed and glared from under her shawl.

"No, we're set up at Mrs. Carr's and we'll stay there 'til we go to housekeeping I 'spose." She could have added that Ben would just as soon move in with a tribe of Indians in a teepee but that would make Ma feel bad. "Don't forget," she said to appease Ma, "we'll be over for dinner tomorrow if you have room."

Ben just didn't want to be too close to his mother-in-law because he thought there would be a daily battle for control. And Ellen had to acknowledge the wisdom of keeping a little distance between two such painfully honest and strongly convinced people. Ben hated to be penned in, and Ellen admired the way he thought things out and stuck to his plans.

"Melie, you keep his head out of this weather, you hear?" Eliza began to badger the black girl, her own slave she was lending the Hedricks as a nurse. You had to help young people, she believed, especially young people like Ellen and Benjamin who'd been exposed to heaven knew what kind of wild ideas.

She began to move on. "Come on by after you get your letter. Selina's sitting in by the parlor fire. Guess her visit with you didn't get her so set up for living outdoors the way it did some folks."

"Good-bye, Ma," Ellen called after her. After turning down Henderson Street, they arrived at the post office.

Before she asked, she knew there was no letter. Mr. Knowles' face told her. Then he shook his head and said, "I'm sorry, Miss Ellen, I don't have a letter from that husband of yours." She was immediately busy with the effort not to cry. A professor's wife with baby and nurse in tow just couldn't burst into tears in the post office. And so she didn't, even when he offered, "Maybe tomorrow."

She had to pray for strength to get out the words, "Thank you,

Mr. Knowles." Pity was hard to bear, even when it was unspoken.

Coming out of the post office, she could hear the stage pounding down Franklin Street just around the corner. Melie rushed ahead with Johnnie so that he could see the horses being driven up the front of the Eagle Hotel with as much as a flourish as the driver could muster considering the heavy load. The post office loungers came out too.

Ellen didn't rush. This coach didn't usually carry mail. Thus it was that Melie was the first to see him. "Yon he is!" she yelled. "Yon he is, Miss Ellen."

And Ellen was in his arms. Everything was all right again. Except for the tears, which gushed freely.

"Now what do tears mean, Mrs. Hedrick?" He embraced her as completely as their winter coats allowed, feeling warm enough to shed his own.

"Oh, Ben," was all she could manage. Governor Swain was coming along with his package, and his face was alight too. Ellen allowed herself to be released from Ben's arms in which she could have rested endlessly.

"Welcome home, Professor," the Governor said. "We're mighty glad you're here." The two men shook hands with great cordiality. "But I reckon' there're some others even gladder." And he moved on with a tip of his hat.

"Good ol' Warping Bars," Ben murmured, "I always thought he

was a real friend."

Then he spoke to Melie and plucked Johnnie from her arms, ignoring her warning cry, "Look out, Mistuh Ben, don't let no snow get on his head." He threw his son into the snowy air, sending the cover flying. Johnnie crowed with glee.

As they walked to their apartment at Mrs. Carr's, the snow stopped falling. A stray fragment from a Psalm flitted into Ben's awareness. "The lines have fallen unto me in pleasant places." How could life have a happier prospect in a better place?

Coming in the opposite direction was a shabby black man they recognized. It was Moses Horton, the poet. As they met, Ben thought Moses looked much older and sadder than he had the last time he saw him. "What you want to come back here for, Mistuh Ben?" he asked. Ben supposed Moses, a free Negro, figured they should have stayed up North.

"Why not, Moses?" he asked. "Seems like a good place, my old college town and all that." He looked closely at Moses' face while Johnnie gabbled, "Da, Da." Moses had written many courting poems for students through the years. Ben wondered if anyone had ever really known the man - other than by reputation.

But no time now. "Good to see you, Moses."

"Yessir, Mistuh Ben." He walked on as the Hedrick procession approached the gate in front of Mrs. Carr's house.

Ellen said softly, "Poor Moses. His book was published so many years ago, and he's still writing love poems to order for the students. Not much of a life, I guess. Maybe he is in the wrong part of the country." She looked up at Ben and he nodded as he opened the door to their temporary home.

By the time the second term began, the Department of Chemistry Applied to Agriculture and the Arts was ready for students in the basement of the fine new building, Smith Hall. The bronze corn sheaves on the capitals in front seemed apropos for the new courses. Ben had installed the new equipment he'd brought from New York. Now students from the country areas could marvel at its strangeness and anticipate learning to use it.

From the college catalogue, students knew they would study "Analytical Chemistry and its applications to the analysis of soils, manures, mineral waters, the assaying ores, the testing of drugs and medicines." The textbooks ordered were also lined up on shelves and included such titles as *Analytical Chemistry* by Roses, *Field Lectures* by Stoddard, *Testing With The Blowpipe* by Plattner, and *Medical Chemistry* by Bowman. Professor Hedrick looked around with pride and hope.

His co-worker, Professor Phillips, was pleased too. Things seemed to be in order for the new endeavor. Just so long as his former student stuck to his subject and didn't get off on religion or slavery, all would go well. A good number of students had registered for the course. Charles hoped Benjamin Hedrick appreciated the opportunity the Lord was sending him with the help of the University, Governor Swain, and himself. He had his apprehensions.

March 1854

Ben and Ellen lay contentedly in their bed at the Carr's house. They were still celebrating the complete delight of being reunited. Being together was everything, everything. The poles of the earth were once more steady now that the stars looked down on them in the same bed.

Having given themselves to each other, they rested in the peace their giving had made and assured each other in soft little sentences and the warmth of side touching side.

"I thought you'd never get here, Benny, life is so incomplete when you're away."

"I know, my darling, it's the same for me, no matter how exciting the classes and the people were in Cambridge. Wonder if ol' Agassiz and Liz love each other half as much as we do. Not that we care, do we, honey?"

A small cry from the next room. A footstep on the floor. Ben and Ellen listened. Was Johnnie all right? The quiet said Melie had checked and all was well.

"Oh, I forgot to tell you something the Governor mentioned today," Ben said into the warmth of her hair. "Are you quite awake? It might be important."

"Yes, I'm awake," she said, almost asleep.

"Well, the Governor asked me today if I would like to buy the lot at Rosemary and Franklin for our home."

"Oh, Ben, I'm awake now! Isn't that where Hatch's Pond is? The one we used to skate on when the ice was thick?"

"Yes, that's the place, but trust me, I'm positive the pond could be drained and a house built on the higher part of the lot. There are some fine big oaks there too."

"I'm getting goose bumps. Tell him we want it. Does the University own it?"

"Whoa there, little filly, you're going too fast. Yes, the University owns the land and will sell it to us for $300."

"Ben, isn't that an awful lot of money? I mean, that's a quarter of your salary."

"I know, but I reckon it's a fair price for that big lot. I've got some ideas for earning money besides from teaching. And we'd have plenty of room for a garden and a stable, whatever we need." His voice betrayed his excitement. "'Course, we'd have to build just a small house to start."

"Now I'm too excited to sleep." She sat up and stared out the window as if hoping to see the land at the other side of town. She could see herself in a new kitchen, see Ben and golden-haired Johnnie waiting for her to serve them - and in the bedroom, maybe a new baby sleeping.

She heard the deep breathing of sleep beside her and knew she was alone in her meditation for the time being. She lay down and directed herself to sleep. She lay there wide-eyed, too alert with joy to fall into unconsciousness.

Chapter Fifteen

**Chapel Hill
June 1854**

Shepherded by Corney Phillips, Ellen and Selina headed down the steep slope of Hillsborough Road. The three of them walked together but not close together because of their broad-brimmed hats and the broad-beamed skirts of well-worn summer dresses. Each swung a deep-belled basket by its handle.

"I told you we'd have a clear day," Corney said. "A blue sky like this pract'cly obliges pickin' and picnickin', doesn't it?" The taller Corney walked a step ahead of her friends with an air of directing the expedition.

"You're right, Corney," Ellen said. "I'm really glad you planned this outing. Even Ben said it would do me good to get out and leave Johnnie with Melie for a change and go someplace besides our house in-the-making." Her hazel eyes shone in the shadow of her brim. She felt light-hearted and light-headed from the sweetness of honeysuckle blooming along the ditches.

"Well," Selina said, "Nobody told me it would do any good except myself. But I like a good hen party where we can speak our minds." She flung out her free arm. "Sort of restores your soul to get out in the Lord's own world, doesn't it?"

"Law, Sis Lina, I didn't know you were so pious - that's Ellen's bent - but you're right." Corney stopped and the other two bunched up behind her. She gestured towards the woods and fields below them. "The Lord is in his holy temple, let all the earth keep silence before him." In the silence a mockingbird sang a small waterfall of melody. "*Laus Deo*," she added, unable to suppress her superior classical education.

Then Corney whistled - two high notes and a low one. They waited, back came the notes in perfect repetition. "What fun," said the whistler, adding quickly, "Come on, girls, we won't get our baskets filled doing bird duets."

She led them, braking hard in her old shoes, to the foot of the hill and followed the road to the right. "There's the field where I saw a blackberry hedge blooming awhile back." She pointed, turned a piercing glance of her black eyes to silence any possible rebuttal. "And you know Uncle Ben is going to drive out here with lunch about noon time."

"The best part," Selina said, and the others gave pretend bitter laughs in tribute to Selina's rather broomstick-like figure.

Watching their approach as he peered from behind a huge oak was a black man in dust-colored clothes. His fingers were stained from the blackberries, which had been his lunch, his first food since arriving here with the dawn. He groaned inwardly at the interference. He would do his best to stay out of the sight of these white women. He had to wait for dark to get onto the road again, couldn't risk being taken so close to the Underground station at New Garden.

He splashed through the creek and into the woods behind before they could catch sight of him, he hoped.

When the women had struggled up the weed-covered sandy slope from the road, they set down their baskets and donned gloves. Then they spread out, directed by Corney, of course, and began to pick the berries from briar-guarded branches.

Cornelia worked hard at picking, as she did at everything. She moved rapidly through a bush, stripping it of its darkest berries, leaving the red and the green for a later picker or for the birds to finish. Selina and Ellen were slower. Selina picked a few, then stopped to study a butterfly, yellow with black writing, who was visiting some Queen Anne's lace. She crushed a ripe berry as she grasped it too hard. This was a peculiar thing to be doing. The others weren't noticing.

Ellen worked steadily. She put aside the glimpse she'd had of a running black man; must have been somebody's servant sent to gather berries. But why had he run? The others hadn't seen him. Forget it, don't scare them with the idea of a runaway slave. She envisioned the pie she would make at Ma's and bring home to Carr's for Ben to enjoy. But Ma wouldn't mind if she used her kitchen to can some pie berries for next winter, too. Oh, she would be so happy when the new house was finished, and she had her own kitchen. She could see the rows of glass jars in her new pantry. She couldn't really be a village girl at play anymore. Her breasts throbbed a little, but skipping a nursing for once in favor of applesauce and mush wouldn't hurt Johnnie.

She stood, stretched the muscles of her back and rubbed at the waist of her old muslin dress. The friendly sun of early morning had turned fierce as it glowered down from the top of the blue-as-blueing sky. Perspiration rolled down every slope of her body, and she could smell herself too. Was there really someone watching from the woods?

After awhile, Corney stood up and called, "Sun's laying a shadow around my feet, noontime." Selina, basket half-filled, was ahead of the others as they made their way back to the road.

And there was faithful Uncle Ben with the bay hitched to the Phillips' small wagon. Corney hailed him from a distance, and he took off his wrinkled old hat. "Here's yo' dinner, Miss Corney," he called in his thin voice. "Missus and Dilsey done it for you." He gave them a big, largely toothless smile as they reached the wagon and began to take out the contents. "Evenin', Miss Ellen, Miss Lina," he greeted them politely. They responded and asked about Aunt Dilsey who was pronounced "Tol'bul."

"Here, Selina, you're so hungry, carry this pan - looks like pie to me," ordered Corney, handing it to her. "Ellen, you may carry the lemonade jar and I'll bring the rest," she said and accepted the large blue-checked cloth covered package from Uncle Ben. The filled berry baskets were placed in his care.

"Thank you, Uncle Ben," she said. "You may return in about two hours time, we ought to be full and rested by then."

"Yessum, Miss Corney, but kin I ast you somethin'?" Ben's dark face wore a puzzled expression.

"Certainly, Ben, what is it?" She was kind but condescending.

"Why fo' you ladies want to set outdoors and eat?" He stepped back, surprised by his own boldness.

"We just like to sometimes, enjoy the things around us while we eat."

He scratched his gray-grizzled head and smiled. "I'll be back t'rectly then, Miss Corney." He clucked to Dan and headed back up the hill with a thud of horseshoes on the soft dirt road.

The ladies carried their burdens down the road past the blackberry patch until they came to a wide creek - wide, that is, for a creek in the dry month of June. Corney didn't have to direct their way to the familiar spot in blessed shade.

Here broad flat boulders lined the stream and waving strands of willows made a perfect picnic spot. The clear, barely moving water was tranquilizing. They lay down and dipped water onto their dusty faces and swished their hands in the creek. The napkins Mrs. Phillips had sent made good towels.

The lunch was enough for the three plus any group of hikers that might happen by. The blue-checked cloth was spread on the rock to serve as both seat and table. Corney unloaded a plate of still-warm, fragrant fried chicken, biscuits with tips of ruddy ham protruding, a jar of pickled peaches and one of cabbage slaw. Ellen helped undo the silverware and small plates. She set out tin cups for the lemonade and spoke a blessing, hurrying a little to beat Corney to the task. She prayed silently for the figure she'd seen running. The hungry pickers fell to and then still had room for the apple pie Sis Lina had carried.

It was so juicy and buttery that it had fallen into chunks, but no one minded.

When they had stuffed themselves, they lay happily on the warm rock shaded by the overhanging wands of the willow. "Seems far away, doesn't it?" Corney asked.

"Away from what," Lina wanted to know.

"Home, everything."

"Not really, not like I felt to be really far from home," Ellen observed. How did the place feel to a runaway, her heart asked.

Corney closed that. "Well, you're back now, to stay. Back where we can go blackberry picking every summer. Long as we're all here, that is." She sat up. "What am I saying?"

She had their attention. "This seems like a good time for me to tell you girls something, and it's a secret, really."

"Oh, good, I love a secret, the best talk there is sitting around a table - even a rock table."

"You're a tease, Selina, but I trust you anyway, and besides, wild horses couldn't keep me from telling you, my good friends."

Selina and Ellen felt happy to hear this, since sometimes, Corney's higher education gave her such a superior air, they weren't sure of their standing with her. They forgave her for having a professor father who saw to it that she got as much education as her brothers even though she couldn't be enrolled as a student, naturally. Ellen's taste of higher learning at Edgeworth made her a little envious, she had to admit. But Corney was ready to tell all.

Ellen primed her. "Tell us then, Corney. I think I could guess, but I'd rather hear you say it."

"Well, hush then, Ellen, and let her tell us."

The black eyes looked hypnotically into theirs. "Magnus Spencer has asked me to marry him."

Ellen and Selina gasped and reached over to hug Cornelia and her momentous news. Giggles and laughs bound the fragments of exclamations. She went on, "Papa consents. Now what do you think of your Old Maid friend?"

Selina gushed, "Well, of course he wants you to marry him. Ellen, you weren't here last Commencement to see the eyes he had for her. That big senior from Alabama was wrapped up in Corney like she was the one giving out the diplomas."

"I'm so happy for you, Corney," Ellen said, kissing her. "And you're not an Old Maid. Margaret Fuller was almost forty years old before her head allowed her heart to rule." Then she worried she had said too much, Corney being four years her senior.

But Corney threw back her head and laughed. "Exactly, I'm just finding out how beautiful life can be." She lifted her lemonade cup in tribute.

"Tell us, then, what are your plans - yours and Magnus'?"

"Well, we don't have them yet, but when he has his law practice built up down there in Clinton, we'll be married up here - maybe next June. And then we'll live down there in Alabama."

"Oh, Corney, you'll be leaving Chapel Hill," moaned Selina.

"I know, but you go where your lover goes, right, Ellen?"

"How well I know, you can't be happy any other way. And besides you'll certainly be coming back here to visit, won't you? And you won't be going for a long time. Oh. I'm so glad for you, honey. May you be as happy as Ben and I."?

Corney actually had a mist across her eyes. "So do I. You are quite an example of matrimonial bliss - and you know we'll visit. Think of Mama and Papa, they'll have to see their only girl-child sometimes.

And then we can go on more outings like this." She sighed. "I wonder if women in other places find it as hard to leave them as I will Chapel Hill."

They could see Ben and the wagon out on the road and gathered up the picnic materials. Ellen had formed a plan and carried it out as Corney and Selina turned to leave. She untied her stained apron, its deep pocket filled with chicken and ham biscuits, and placed the apron carefully on a flat rock, while pretending to tie her shoe. "God help him," she prayed.

She'd have a lighter conscience whether or not the man found the food. How pitiful to be in flight and hunted. She could say she supposed the apron fell off in the field if they noticed it was gone.

The man in the woods waited until he was sure the women had gone before he ventured out to pick up the package.

Chapter Sixteen

Summer 1855

The Hedrick house was soon built, a small house on a large lot now drained of its pond. There was some murmuring that Professor Hedrick had made a mistake in cutting his house off from Franklin Street. Franklin was both Pall Mall and Bond Street to Chapel Hill, but murmurs usually went on to admit that perhaps the reason for the house's placement was the slope of the land downward toward Franklin. Actually the land was on the tip of a plateau which contained the village. Theirs was the last house, except for the shacks of several free Negroes, on the way to Raleigh and the east from the center of the village. Thus the Hedrick House was a bit removed from the comings and goings of the college community.

Ellen felt everything about their house was just right. She was almost but not quite in sight of Ma's and that was right. Though Corney had departed in newlywed state in June, it was still good to have both Phillips families - Charles' and his father's as neighbors - not to mention the Swains. The campus itself stretched back from the other side of Franklin and the stores were mostly further toward Columbia Street. All convenient, she didn't have to take a coach to do her errands as in Cambridge.

She was fairly sure there were more murmurs - the price you paid for the joy of living in a small place - when Ben decided to have a room added to the house the summer before their second baby was born. The room had nothing to do with the expected baby, that is, it wasn't for the baby; it was a study for his father. With the glad noise of two-year-old Johnnie, Ben could already see the need for a place of refuge. He acted on the problem in good weather.

At the same time he acted on a theory he'd accepted and heard of being carried out in other areas. A six-sided structure has extra strength not possessed by one with just four sides. The basic unit built by bees is a hexagon, a six-sided cell. He never tired of explaining this to workmen as they built the room, or to the curious of all ages as they came to see for themselves. The summer of 1855 in Chapel Hill starred Professor Hedrick's Honeycomb Room. Wags among the townsfolk smirked, "What can you expect? He's got more learnin' than a body needs."

Ellen didn't mind very much the long climb - about 200 yards - down to the spring for water. Usually she didn't have to do the fetching herself; Melie brought up the water unless Aide, Belle or Henry from Ma's house filled the bucket, which stood on the back porch. It was comfortable to have family close by.

Any inconveniences were minor compared to the feeling that this was the right place to be. Probably the discomfort that they felt at first to be back where slavery was a part of life – probably that would pass. For now they would follow Professor Phillips' lead and keep such feelings to themselves. This wasn't easy, but, the two of them had a pact.

It was gratifying to be close to people she was naturally close to. Besides Ma and Selina and the others, and poor ol' Pa out at Rock Springs, she liked being in frequent touch with friends such as the Mitchell girls. It was pleasant to visit and be visited, to be a part of the Sewing Club, to walk to church not far from Ma's, to stores or the post office, giving and receiving news along the way. Never mind that the stores in Boston had goods Mr. Carr never dreamed of; Ben could shop up north for her. He was good-natured about taking orders; half the village was getting lists ready for his return trip to the North at semester break. Being the wife of Professor Hedrick, as well as the former Mary Ellen Thompson, gave her status she enjoyed.

November 1855

Her chair in the parlor was placed so that she could see out across the lawn while she nursed the baby. This mid-November day was especially fine so that Johnnie could play in the fallen leaves to his heart's content. She watched him pile the dimming gold and brown leaves and roll in them. Melie sat close by on a bench she'd improvised from saw horses left from construction. She was probably humming; she was like a kettle with her humming. Knowing that added to the placid feeling the scene gave Ellen, now a month past childbirth

The little warm head fitted into crook of her arm, and the warmer little mouth fitted over her nipple and worked. A gentle sensation.

Precious. Thank you, Lord. Charlie - Charles Joseph, named for Professor Charles Phillips - had come into the world more easily than Johnnie had. Still she had again that resigning to pain, then in limpness, rejoicing in new life. Most second babies come easier, Ma said, but Ellen thought her own state of mind had something to do with it. Johnnie has arrived in faraway Cambridge. With this birth, surrounded by loving faces - Ma, Dr. Jones, as well as Ben and Selina, of course, she'd had familiarity.

She smiled at the tiny plink of her milk landing in Charlie's empty stomach. From ravenous to replete in a few minutes, that's a new baby.

Footsteps. While she dreamed, the playing field had emptied. In came the players - the rosy-faced little boy and his nurse, faithful dark Melie who looked bothered.

"He's still too little!" Johnnie shouted accusingly as he ran past Ellen and Charlie.

"Johnnie, you hush now, you gone scare you li'l brother while he having dinner," Melie told him. "I'm sorry, Miss Ellen, Johnnie bound to come in ar'ter his other ball."

"It's all right, Melie, " Ellen said, "I don't want Johnnie feeling put out of the house because of Charlie."

"Well, I tried, like you tol' me, but..."

Charging back, Johnnie in his frayed shoes. He stopped beside her, her first man-child, his sunny hair level with the bald pate of Charlie who was still working...

"Come on then, Johnnie, you got you ball," Melie urged, taking his plump hand.

But he had a question. "Mama, will Charlie ever finish eating on you?"

She laughed softly. "I wouldn't be surprised. You did, you know. I expect he'll be playing outdoors with you this time next year."

When the door closed behind them, Ellen's window view enclosed Ben coming home, coming across the front yard, and her heart pulsed with gladness. With his dark head up, he looked straight ahead and walked with the quick steps of a man who'll be happy to get where he's going. Although he looked small beneath the tall trees - he was just a few inches taller than Ellen - his bearing radiated confidence born of success, she thought.

He stopped to hug Johnnie but didn't stay to toss him in the air. She sensed more haste than usual and resolved to remain relaxed at least as long as it took Charlie to finish his meal.

His steps on the porch made little beats of anticipation in her. His beaming smile as he came in, his "Hello, my love," picked up the tempo. She lifted her face for his kiss and felt the familiar and stimulating roughness of his moustache.

He stepped back and regarded her, all rosy and golden with Charlie's pink dome at her breast and the afternoon light discovering them. "Now that would make a painting nice enough for a museum," he said. "Makes me happy just to see you and our little fellow. Would have been home earlier, but I have to watch the students and make sure they clean up the equipment and put it where it belongs."

"I know, sweetheart. Did you have a good day?"

"It was all right, considering what went on last night - the effigy burning. Did you hear about it?"

"No, guess Ma hasn't had the time to come tell me. Must have been small potatoes or she'd have found the time."

"Not such small potatoes, considering the victim."

"Not Governor Swain, I hope."

"No, this time it was Charles Phillips, and he was that nervous and angry today! I spent a good deal of time just trying to calm him down."

"Oh, Lord help us! What were the students off on Professor Phillips about? I'm glad Corney's not here!"

"It was something about the grades he gave the engineering students. 'Professor Phillips Unfair,' the sign at the burning said. I 'spect maybe he's too rough on some of those boys - it's their first year, at least for some of them."

"Seems like they were just looking for an excuse for a frolic. Ma's said all along students just don't like Charles Phillips, but you can't always go by what Ma says."

"True, but there's usually some truth in it, in what she overhears in her dining room. Oh well, no harm done except to make ol' Charlie more red in the face and crosser than ever."

"Well, his namesake isn't a bit like him." She smiled down at the baby as he slacked in his work.

"Thank the Lord for that. What I am afraid of is that the 'persecution' will bring out the preacher in him with me as the object. He can go on and on at me, how I have got to keep quiet on what I think about slavery and creationism. You know how he picked up on the influences that were so different for us up North. He thinks I am going to let it all out someday, but I don't feel so pent up as that. If we shut down on being able to speak freely somewhere, we're in bad shape.

Ellen moved the sleeping Charlie away from her breast and handed him to his father, then buttoned her bodice. "You've got to get along with him, honey," she said, rising to stretch her legs. "But I know it makes you mad to have to watch every word - 'specially when you're somewhere besides the classroom. It's not as if you taught anything but chemistry during class."

"Exactly, you do understand, Ellen. Everybody 'round here must know I don't go spreading my thoughts on anything political, except to you and a few friends. That's a teacher's integrity, I'd say, not use your position with students to preach your own gospel."

"Yes sir, Professor." She reached for the baby, kissed his downy head, and carried him to his cradle.

Chapter Seventeen

**Chapel Hill
December 27, 1855**

"Good-bye, my dear," Julia Phillips said to Ellen as they stood by the Hedrick's front door. "You're holding up well. Mr. Hedrick will be back from Boston before you know it. You're a brave girl, and I'm glad you had a nice Christmas, you and your sweet babies."

The older woman embraced the younger, giving her a powdery little kiss.

"And, I'm glad he has you to cool down any hot abolitionism he might catch up north," she whispered into Ellen's ear before saying good-bye again and leaving quickly.

Zing. The whisper had caught Ellen thinking Mrs. Phillips was so gracious you'd never know she wasn't a born Southerner. "Come back soon, Mrs. Phillips," she called after her automatically. "I'll see you tomorrow night." She was smiling and being the gracious young matron. She watched as her visitor made her way down the path, looking like a walking hand-bell with her heavy skirts swinging to where Uncle Ben and her carriage waited out on Franklin Street.

"Mama, Mama!" Johnnie burst out of the back room where Melie had kept him confined.

Ellen turned and saw a miniature man dressed in his father's beaver hat and a coat which dragged the floor. "I'm going to N'York on the cars!" the pygmy told her.

"All right then, sir, step right this way," she said, waving him into a chair. His eyes twinkled, stars of delight. "Sit right here, sir. Ticket, please."

With no intention of cooling down any political fever he might catch, since there was no danger, Ellen sat down that evening to write her favorite correspondent. Sitting at her little desk in the parlor, she picked a new nib for her pen, rested it, and began:

> *Thursday, 8 1/2 p.m.,*
> *Dec. 27, 1855*

> *My dear husband,*

> *I commence writing early tonight. Aide isn't here, nor Melie, and Johnnie and Charlie are both asleep so the house is quiet as a mouse. This morning I received yours of Monday. I thank you for being so considerate of me and preparing so well for Sunday. I was happy to get the Star papers. I hope you found the Agassiz lectures interesting.*

> *Do get one of those thick woolen comforters and wrap*

it well around my "old man's" throat. I wouldn't have it kept sore for anything. You must take extra care since I am not along to nurse and sympathize with you in your days of ennui [work at the Naval Almanac].

I have collected your nine letters and shall answer them in full....

... A bunch of celery too, the "old woman" would like. You mustn't forget my fruitcake. Eat one big dinner for me at the Brattle House.

Can you send Johnnie a pair of shoes by mail? His are so ragged that I have to keep him in the house all the time and he almost runs me out, he keeps up such a racket...

...The darkies are gay and lively. Melie has more invitations out than I have. Old Mrs. Phillips was here this afternoon and invited me to meet a few friends at her house tomorrow night. I promised to go, to take Melie with me to keep harm away. She wishes you would see her relatives in New York.

Johnnie says bring him a "colty"...

When do you turn your face homeward? Be mindful of ice and snow if you travel all the way to New York on the cars.

Dr. Mitchell was here last evening to inquire about you. Charles Phillips was here while I was uptown. Melie said he had a letter in his hand, I wish I had seen it. We had considerable fun Christmas. Ma wants me to give a big dinner. Good Night!

Your wife, your own dear wife

She kissed the place where she had signed her name, blotted the last sheet, and folded the letter to fit its envelope. She wouldn't seal it until tomorrow in case there was news to be added. She was glad to have finished what she set out to do. Cambridge wives could just walk in the stores and buy what they wanted - dishes, furnishings, cloth, furs. Maybe North Carolina, maybe even Chapel Hill, would offer that abundance of manufacturers stuff someday, but for now Ben would just have to be the shopper. He was so generous to take time for shopping away from tracking the planets and studying the substance of life. The extra assignment made possible these purchases.

Ben. It seemed so long since he'd boarded the stage for Hillsborough. Longing swept over her, and she let herself feel it. The room had grown cold. No Melie to keep the fire going. Praise God they had a house of their own.

She pulled her shawl closer around her and went into Ben's study in the dark. She was beginning to like the odd, six-sided shape he admired so much. Moonlight through the long windows was so bright she could almost read the titles of Ben's books. He was such a truth-seeker, and that part of him she couldn't always understand; yet she was awed by his constant thirst for knowledge.

It was God who was Truth, and He was very real to Ellen. God was God to Ben, too, yet...maybe Ben was growing closer to the Creator by looking deeply into His Creation. After all, what he learned about the stars and the gases was a way of learning about the Father, even though the folks at the Presbyterian Church didn't seem to see it that way. Ellen was serene because she actually felt the presence of God within her, within Ben and the children, saw Him at work in their lives, trusted him utterly.

She let her forehead touch the cold glass of the window beside his desk. She believed the Father inspired her husband to know and weigh and test the elements he taught his students about. If she could keep him close enough, her sense of the Almighty would be given to him too, as their bodies gave each other their deepest selves.

She pictured the moonlight touching Ben's room so far up north. Their Father's nightlight was blessing them both.

The young woman's happiness, her plans for the comfort of their household were not conscious of the forces of injustice and fear which would stifle them before the new year was ended.

Chapter Eighteen

With Ben home again and classes back in session, the household was ready to resume its normal happy hum, but two events were to be forerunners of the doom awaiting normalcy.

One dark afternoon at the end of January, Ellen stopped in at Ma's on her way home from Carr's where she had picked up some of the fancy soap, which Charlie's delicate skin seemed to prefer. She found Selina doing some mending before the fire in the little parlor so filled with fond memories.

They had just begun to chat about Johnnie's pride in his new shoes "from the train" when Eliza burst in from the back of the house.

"Whew!" she breathed as she dropped without mercy onto a little parlor chair. "What did happen, Ellen? Go on and tell us!"

Selina took the cue. "Yes, Ellen, you know we're dying to know what the boarders were whispering about."

Ellen had to laugh. If you can't laugh when you feel like it, what does it mean to be at home? "You all are so funny. It's nothing you need to be bothered about, I'd say."

"Well, if we knew about it, we could judge that for our selves, couldn't we?" Ma would have made a good lawyer, Ellen thought, not for the first time.

Ma went on, "What we want to know is why were the senior boarders an hour late to dinner yesterday? And when they came they weren't paying much attention to the food but muttering to each other something about their rights." Selina nodded her agreement.

"Why, Little Dumps' chicken pies were cold when Andrew and Stuart and the others came! "T'wasn't our fault, of course, but I was still ashamed, not up to my standard a'tall."

Ellen sobered. "Well, I guess it's no secret since two meetings were held - the senior class and the faculty. Monsieur Harrisee came by to walk over with Ben. He likes us, you know, doesn't have any friends in the village, and he's really nice about helping me with speaking French..."

"Ellen, you're off the subject," Selina reminded her. She had put down the shirt with the needle tucked in.

Ma, too, was hanging on Ellen's next words.

Ellen repressed a sense of pleasure at knowing something they very much wanted to know. She tried not to engage in gossip but didn't see how it could hurt to tell about what happened. "Well, it seems like the seniors were making plans here in January for Commencement in June. Don't know what all they planned, but the fly in the ointment was this: they voted to invite a Catholic bishop, Archbishop Hughes of New York to be their baccalaureate preacher."

"A Catholic priest! Well, that is a shocker," Ma said.

Selina added, "Uh-oh."

"What threw Governor Swain was that the seniors took a vote, wrote and mailed their invitation without so much as a by-your-leave. There was fast work going on here. The Governor got wind of it somehow and showed up at their next meeting to lecture them. Then he called a faculty meeting the evening of the very same day and repeated his lecture. You'd think the seniors had invited the devil to preach to them." She filled the corners of the parlor with her ringing laugh.

Eliza sat back now, her hands on her skirt with knees apart. "Might as well have asked the Old Boy, I 'spect, in the view Governor Manley and all the other old Whigs. And maybe it's even worse when you look at the new Know-Nothing party. Mr. Wheat says that crowd is death to Catholics 'cause all the immigrants, the Irish and all, are Catholic and push regular Americans out of jobs." There was agreement in her little squinted eyes.

Selina remarked, "Land sakes, Ma, I didn't know you knew all that! I'd of thought the students were having fun and knew they were putting their foot in it inviting a priest down here where most folks have never seen a priest, or even a Catholic." She patted the curl trained to lie on her cheek. "'Course, when I was up north, I met plenty of 'em - like that Miz Murrett and her daughter. Nice as could be, weren't they, Ellen?"

"Yes, they are, and Ben and I did meet a lot of Catholics, not so much in Cambridge as in Boston - in the stores and all. But that's not North Carolina. People here are - you know we're mostly Presbyterian and Baptist, some Methodists with a sprinkle of Episcopalians and Lutherans, Ben's family, you know." She couldn't help thinking provincial, that's what they are here, the Governor and all.

She went on, "Well, when Monsieur Harrisee and Ben came in after the faculty meeting, the Frenchman said he'd been well entertained. Ben wasn't laughing it off so much since he didn't like to see Governor Swain so upset."

Eliza and Selina gave their nods here, both knowing Ben was indebted to their neighbor, the college president. "So what did the Governor say to the professor?" Eliza wanted to know.

"Well, Ben says the Governor first talked about not being disturbed by the religious consideration, how he reminded them he'd voted for religious freedom when the state constitution was revamped. What he's bothered about is the politics, the reaction in Raleigh and all over the state if such a speaker were to actually appear at Commencement."

"Yes, he would be," Eliza said. "He's always been one to bend to popular opinion."

"Don't forget, he's our friend, Ma," Ellen insisted. "Anyway, the Governor told them the invitation should never have been sent because of what's happening this presidential election year. Ma hit it when she said the Know-Nothings would be put off since they are trying to save the country from low-paid Catholic labor. Seems like some of the big men down here are on that side, even if we don't have the immigrant situation, it's a way of not coming down either for or against slavery. Guess they figure it's the best we can do to keep things as they are in the South."

It's too much for me to take in," Selina observed. She picked up the dingy white shirt and resumed her mending.

"Well, you all wanted to hear. It nothing new - the Governor trying to stay on the good side of the legislature and the trustees, too, I reckon. I wouldn't want to be in his shoes. Anyway, Ben thinks he lives in fear of being labeled unfavorable to the big planters with all their slaves down east. Said he brought in all his courtroom skills and seemed very defensive."

"I can believe that, honey," Eliza said, getting up. "Thanks for satisfying our curiosity. Come back when you can," she said as she went out.

Selina looked up from her work and asked, "So how's little Charlie's rash?"

That night with the babies asleep and Melie watching over them,

Ben and Ellen sat in their new chairs just arrived from New York. They felt very much the responsible householders now that they had been able to return some of the furniture Ma had loaned them. Their own home, their own furniture - it was so satisfying. Perhaps the smug feelings were mostly Ellen's since Ben didn't think of such things except when she reminded him. Not that he didn't feel blessed but that he was usually preoccupied planning lectures.

Tonight, however, he had another agenda. He'd waited until this quiet time with the clock ticking and the fire burning so agreeably.

"Ellen, love, I've got something good to tell you about."

She turned to him and smiled. "Then, do."

He picked up a paper and handed it to her. In the lamplight she read its name, *The Carolina Cultivator* She looked at him inquiringly. *The Carolina Cultivator.* That's the farmers' paper, isn't it?"

"Yes, Mr. Cooke gets it out in Raleigh, started last spring. I've waited to tell you about my connection, maybe afraid you wouldn't approve."

He took the paper from her and folded it so the lead editorial was framed. "Here, read this, my little wife, and see what you think."

She took the paper again, giving him a slightly accusatory look. She read aloud, "'Beginning in February, there will be a new editor: Benjamin Sherwood Hedrick...' Oh Ben, how wonderful!"

She continued in a tone of pride, "...whose position before the public is such as to make formal introduction unnecessary.' Well, pardon me, I'm impressed. 'As a gentleman of acknowledged talents and a great devotion to the cause of agricultural science, his name and contributions will prove a valuable accession to the merits of *The Carolina Cultivator.*

Her cheeks grew pinker as she exclaimed, "Well, Ben, here let me give you some recognition at home." She went to him and knelt to embrace and kiss him, not daring to burden the new chair with double weight. "At last somebody found out the truth about my husband and put it in print! I'm so happy, darling."

He lifted her to her feet and they enfolded each other before resuming their seats.

He felt lighter and freer now that he'd told her. "Remember when your father said he didn't think science could teach farmers anything?"

"Well," she said, "Rock Spring isn't exactly a center of farming, sweet one."

"True, but Mr. Thompson isn't alone. After all, I grew up in farming country. It's the pride of the farmer to wrest crops from the soil; he can't admit too much advice. That's just it: this paper is flying against a lot of ignorance. I don't know how many farmers might not even know how to read. Guess the well-off planters can read all right, but who knows whether they would read this or not?"

"But Ben," she said, "you'll have to take a positive attitude that some farmers will read and profit, won't you?"

"Oh yes, I am very positive or I wouldn't have taken the job." He rose to spread the blinking red coals before banking the fire for the night.

By April Ellen was especially pleased that the new editor's voice reflected pleasure in two of his worlds coming together. She read, "Experiments in Agriculture...and Who Should Make Them."

> ...we shall have rules drawn from experience, and these will be more valuable when deduced from the combined observations of many farmers...Astronomy is now the most perfect of the sciences. Observation and theory say the same thing. Knowing the principles by which the motion of the stars are regulated, the Astronomer can predict years before-hand where they will at any given time...The empirical laws which had been gained from long continued and numerous observations finally led to the discovery of the general principles which explained the whole...
>
> Other sciences have grown to a high degree of perfection, why should agriculture prove an exception? ...But before we can hope for much to be accomplished, it is first necessary

that farmers become intelligent observers of nature. No single farmer in the narrow limits of his own fields can expect to solve many of the problems connected with his profession, but each may contribute something and receive in return the benefits of the contributions of others.

Ellen was so pleased that Ben was rising to this opportunity to help people such as their own families. And Grandfather Sherwood subscribed and sent his observations from Iowa, along with expression of concern that his namesake might be undertaking more than is good for his "physical being."

Grandfather's forebodings for Ben's future were prophetic, though he mistook the arena of combat.

Chapter Nineteen

Chapel Hill
Summer 1856

During the summer, Ben looked forward to Superintendent Calvin Wiley's Education Convention planned for Salisbury in October. He felt honored to be attending as the representative of the University even though the Governor had given him no choice. Not even to Ellen did he admit how much he would like being seen as important so close to his home territory.

And the week before the Convention, there was to be the State Agricultural Fair in Raleigh. As editor of *The Cultivator* he'd received a special invitation and was running a series of articles to whet the interest of farmers and their wives in entering exhibits ranging from "Jacks and Jennets" to "Needles, Wax, and Shell Work."

But even the busy editor/teacher/scientist found the simmering world of politics intruding as the summer wore on. Party conventions were reported in the newspapers according to the bias of each.

Conflict between the interest of the South and the rest of the country dominated the conventions-and the reporting. Ben's residency in Cambridge had broadened his views, he supposed. He sensed the blindness of his beloved South and the hot defensiveness against any but "safe" views, but enwrapped in his still fresh professional roles, he felt no personal involvement. He observed.

Northern Democrats had long chafed under the federal dominance of Southerners and their maneuvering to support a slave-based agricultural economy. The Democratic Party's exhausted delegates finally compromised on fence-straddling James Buchanan, but many disaffected members defected to the new Republican Party rising in Ohio and Illinois. The Republicans were the abolitionists' delight. They openly opposed slavery and nominated the famous explorer of the West, Colonel John Fremont. A third party, the American or Know-Nothing, avoided a stand on slavery and offered former President Millard Fillmore as its candidate.

News of the anti-slavery party vibrated throughout the South. It was *bete noir* and promptly dubbed Black Republican. Reaction in the South and by most residents of Chapel Hill was that Black Republicans must be headed off, their ticket omitted from ballots in the South. A way of life was at stake.

Ben and Ellen had long been aware of William Holden, a quick-change artist as editor of the *North Carolina Standard* and leader of the state's Democrats. His words still made Ben's blood perk as it had in Cambridge.

The Hedricks watched as King Billy rose to new heights of bombast and sarcasm. Now he had a more immediate enemy than

Harriet Beecher Stowe: the Black Republican party. Its ticket must not be listed on the ballot in North Carolina. Now Holden was on the alert to drive home the terrible fate awaiting anyone so foolhardy as to express approval of the Black Republican candidates. He was delivered a juicy plum.

Political talk filtered in where the people of Chapel Hill gathered that summer. In the post office, the stores, in sewing circles, the buzzing was more animated than usual, particularly after the papers had arrived on the stagecoach. There was swapping of papers, especially among the Phillips and Mitchells and others of Northern-origin - or previous Northern residency, as the Hedricks. The *New York Times* was swapped for Greeley's *Tribune*, *The Greensborough Patriot* (pro Fillmore) for the Raleigh *Standard*(smoking hot for Buchanan). If Garrison's Republican *Liberator* was to be found it was undercover. The small summer contingent of Eliza J.'s boarders was as full of talk as biscuits.

Ben was receiving a new sheet, courtesy of Grandfather Sherwood who wrote:

"*You appear to be a little surprised that I should anticipate an injury to yourself in receiving a paper such as The Valley Whig. An offense no greater exiled a worthy citizen from Virginia quite recently...No greater offense did exile Crooks and McBride from your state about the time John Sherwood was threatened with mob law by the respectable citizens of Guilford...But from your remarks, I trust that the Society among whom you associate are not to be counted among such 'respectable citizens.'*

Surely Grandfather Sherwood was being overly cautious. Ben reflected that one reason Grandfather had left the state was to get out of a slave society. From deep memory Ben seemed to hear again the clack of leg irons on Lock's Bridge, the sight of those driven slaves and their brave singing.

He did a lot of listening to the political talk in town and wasn't surprised to hear himself speculate that maybe it was time for a new party. He felt himself really threatened during the campaign, for the first time.

When the new term started in August, his chemistry class claimed most of his attention when he wasn't at home with Ellen and the babies.

But he continually felt some inner stresses with the dark memories and the Cambridge insights firming his conscience like one of Father's brick walls. It was disquieting, and it was so for Ellen, too, since she was so sensitive to his weather.

She had asked him how the church could find slavery immoral up North but a blessing founded on scripture in the South. For an answer he had kissed her.

The time of the presidential primary drew near.

August 7

"How can I tie your shoe unless you hold still?" Ellen held Johnnie on her lap as he wiggled and struggled. He was so eager to get outside and play with Katie from next-door that he was like a bunch of fishing worms.

Ben contributed a kiss on the top of her head on his way out. "Bye, honey, I'm on my way to the polls before class takes up. Behave yourself for Mama now, Johnnie."

"Good-bye, sweetheart, see you at dinner-time." She put Johnnie down, and he shot out past his father. She stood at the front door for a moment and let her eyes follow Ben out to the road. He had a quick gait, not like his father's and hers, not a farmer's lope. Thanks, Lord, for arranging things so that Ben can be where learning is the concern. She admired his erect, purposeful carriage.

Reaching Franklin Street, Ben continued his brisk pace toward the center of the village where not much else was on the move. Most voters for the primary were not yet out, he supposed. The rising heat of the August day simmered beneath the cool of the overarching trees. Aunt Dilsey, white-aproned, was sweeping the Phillips' front porch. The college looked peaceful across the way. He saw Eliza J. nearing

Carr's store but didn't hurry to catch up with her. Why should he intercept the busy boardinghouse keeper on her rounds?

"Howdy, Professor, 'Morning, Professor", "How're you today. Professor Hedrick?" "Nice day for the primary." Ben was greeted by fellow townsmen and some students, some old enough to vote, he supposed.

Entering the post office, he smiled his grave smile, howdied everyone, signed in with Mr. Graves, the registrar, and received his ballot and marked it.

He moved to turn the paper in at the window, and Couzart, a student he knew, leaned over and scanned it. This was annoying, but Ben said nothing.

Couzart smiled and said, "I see you voted Democratic too. That's all right, Professor," "How are you today, Professor Hedrick?"

Ben nodded and turned to leave the dark little room that was the Chapel Hill post office. From the clump of students in the doorway, someone hailed him before he could get through. He needed to get over to Smith and set up the equipment for today's lab experiment.

One of the young men blocked his way, put a hand on Ben's sleeve and asked, "Say, Professor, how did you vote?"

Restraining his annoyance, Ben allowed he'd voted for the Democratic ticket.

"Well," the fellow pressed, "are you for Buchanan for president in

November, or not?"

"Well, gentlemen," Ben answered, a little proud to have his choice asked, "All things considered, especially since I am not a proponent of the extension of slavery into the new states, I really wish there would be a Fremont ticket so I could vote for the Pathfinder."

"Really?" the boy asked loudly. "Did I hear you right? You'd vote for a Black Republican?"

Ben had the feeling that every ear in the post office was taking in his words, but he repeated his assertion. "Yes, I'd vote for the Republican's man, Colonel Fremont, if he's on the ballot, but I kind of doubt he will be. I like what I know of the man."

Mullens, one of those Ben knew, pushed the subject. "Well if you'd vote for that Northern party, does that mean you wouldn't support the South if the North attacked us?"

The post office ear leaned in. Ben cleared his throat. "Of course not, I am of the South and for the South." Warming up, he continued, "And if any outside force attacked the South, we would all fight together; we'd be a unit."

A figure emerged from the darkness within, staggering a little and emitting a strong smell of alcohol, an election day celebrant. Ben recognized Everett who was still fighting the Mexican War, though returned from it some time ago. "Way a mint," he asked Ben. "Jus lemme tell you a thing or two 'bout fighting. Yah see, it's thish way.

The rich folks gets in a fuss 'bout their prop'ty and sends the poor folks to fight for it. I ain't plannin' to go to no war to save no rich man's nigger slaves for him, I can tell you that fo'sho."

Ben was embarrassed to be the center of such a scene. He tried to quiet the drunken man but Everett wasn't through.

"lemme tell you this fo'sho', Professor. When I volunteered to go, there was a lot of rich fellows put their names down too, but soon's the Company was made up. Didn't see them or their names anymore."

"Oh well, Everett, maybe that happened sometimes, but it seems to me all kinds of folks did their parts well in Mexico."

The doorway block broke open to let Everett, still mumbling about not fighting for rich folks, through. Ben followed and hurried toward Smith building, feeling a little put out by the delay he'd experienced at the polls. Today he wanted to conduct an experiment from Plattner's "Testing with a Blowtorch."

That night Ellen became tense and a little uneasy on hearing what had happened at the post office, but they made the decision to put it out of their minds.

Several days passed before the Democrats' primary victory was known. Meanwhile the students showed a bit of recklessness, typical of election time hijinks. The President decided to assign campus patrol duty to tutors and some faculty members.

The way Ben heard it from Fetter who had patrol duty Saturday night; the fire was a big surprise. Fetter had met only one student on his last round past the belfry at 10:15. He had thought nothing of the little bit of bell ringing and shouting at midnight and was astonished to hear the next morning that the wooden bell tower had burned to the ground. Lucas, a tutor, said he'd seen fireballs tossed at the belfry and heard shouts for Fremont and other candidates.

The entire village went to see what had happened in the night. Ben, Ellen, and Johnnie walked into the deep campus and could smell the disaster before they saw it. Ashes, the belfry was ashes. And the blackened mound of the college bell lay on its side in gray dust.

Who knew if it could ring again?

A few days later
Governor's Office, Raleigh

"I am delighted with this," William Holden said as he handed Governor Bragg the letter he had just received. The bald, bearded Holden could scarcely wait for Bragg to read the letter before telling him why he was so pleased. "You see, it's just what we need to pin the tail on the donkey- Hedrick, that is."

"See what you mean, Holden, see exactly what you mean. This, n the *Standard*, following last week's opener on driving Fremont men out of the state, will be perfect. Just in good time for the campaign."

He clapped his big hands together and smiled with satisfaction. Then

he picked up the letter and said, "Right here he puts his finger on

Hedrick: 'We were very much gratified to notice this article in your

paper at this particular time, for we have been reliably informed that

a professor at our State University is an open and avowed supporter

of Fremont, and declares his willingness - nay, his desire - to support

the Black Republican ticket...if our information is correct...ought he

not be 'required to leave'; at least dismissed from a situation where his

poisonous influence is so powerful?'

Chapter Twenty

Chapel Hill
September 1856

When the Presbyterian Ladies Sewing Circle met in September, Maria Mitchell was hostess and in charge of seeing that everything went smoothly: that the ladies got into no deep discussions nor gossiped too maliciously. Thus when Laura asked whether anyone had seen yesterday's _Standard_ she got the shush sign from Maria and a tilt of the head toward Ellen. Maria hoped Ellen hadn't heard. Laura subsided, realizing after she'd spoken that it was a mistake.

But Ellen had heard. She worked her piece of tatting with great vigor in the silence. She broke the silence with, "I suppose everyone thinks King Billy's proclamation was aimed at Professor Hedrick."

Old Mrs. Mitchell said she'd have Josie bring in some fresh tea. Then Maria ventured bravely, "I thought it was mean. I don't know why Mr. Holden would do such a thing. After all, it's a free country, isn't it?"

"That's right," Sue Battle took up, "Professor Hedrick hasn't tried to hide the fact that he supports Fremont. Professor Battle says a university is a place where people can think differently and still get along. But I don't know why an editor would deliberately try to pick a fight the way Holden is doing. Maybe it will pass, maybe nothing will come of it. I certainly hope so."

"Thank you, Sue," Ellen said. "Benjamin and I feel rather bad about it. It's not as though he's tried to teach his students politics. He never talks politics in chemistry class." She laughed. "He's too busy trying to put over principles and teach them through experiments. If you just knew how he loves his work!"

Maria to the rescue. "I can tell by what my father says. When he approves of a scientist, he approves all the way. He said the editorial is hogwash, that Professor Hedrick doesn't teach politics."

Ellen felt a sense of support from her old friends, even though no one else spoke.

At home she reread the offensive editorial. (1)

Fremont in the South

Can it be possible that there are men in the South who prefer Fremont for the Presidency or who would acquiesce in his election? The New York Herald boasts that there are already Electoral Tickets in Virginia, Kentucky, and Maryland; and it adds, "Texas and North Carolina will probably follow suit." This is a vile slander on the Southern people. No Fremont Electoral Ticket can be formed in North Carolina - mark that! It may be that

*there are traitors here and there in the State, as there were
Tories in the Revolution, who would thus deliver up their
native land to the fury of the fanatic and the torch of the
incendiary; but they are few and far between. They do not
number more than one in one hundred.*

*The election of Fremont would inevitably lead to a
separation of the States. Even if no overt or direct act
of dissolution should take place, our people would never
submit to having their post offices, custom houses and the
like, filled with Fremont's Yankee abolitionists...*

Ellen skipped the part about what the Northern people would
do with Southern "sectional candidates." The last paragraph was the
witch-hunting one.

*If there be Fremont men among us, let them be silenced
or required to leave. The expression of Black Republican
opinions in our midst is incompatible with our honor
and safety as a people. Let our schools and seminaries of
learning be scrutinized; and if Black Republicans can be
found in them, let them be driven out. The man is neither
a fit nor a safe instructor of our young men who even
inclines to Fremont and Black Republicanism.*

She dropped the newspaper in a sprawl on the table, feeling young and frightened. Then she realized Baby Charlie had been in a post-nap roar for some time.

Governor's Office, Raleigh

"You know I believe that, Holden," said Governor Bragg, now forced to look up to meet the glance of the fiery editor. "In these times," he went on, "when a basic unit of our society, the divinely ordained institution of slavery, is being attacked so viciously by those who don't know what it's all about, we have got to keep a firm hold on public opinion. We've got to make a show of unity, most especially about slavery. Why, our whole economy revolves around it." That was pretty good, Bragg thought, maybe Holden could use it in the *Standard.* He stopped to emphasize what had just been said, then he got out his pipe.

Holden took advantage of the break to resume his seat and his message.

"What with you, Governor, as Chairman of the Board of Trustees of the University, how can it miss? That nigger-loving Harvard dandy is going to be heading North."

Bragg hesitated before lighting his pipe. Holden would never be a silk purse, his rough background stuck out. "Whoa, now, Mistuh Editor, watch your language, it might be overheard." He looked around the littered office as if some undetected abolitionist might have wandered in. "All right. So far, so good. Of course, Governor Swain is close to Hedrick, but he knows the good of the college and its supporters come first. Besides, we've got Manley as secretary of the Trustees Executive Committee - and I'm president of it."

That night Ellen felt a little uneasy on hearing what had happened at the post office, but they decided to put it out of their minds.

Several days passed before the Democrats' primary victory was known. Meanwhile the students showed a bit of recklessness, typical of election time hijinks. The president had decided to assign campus patrol duty to tutors and some faculty members.

The way Ben heard it from Fetter who had patrol duty Saturday night, the fire was a big surprise. Fetter had met only one student on his last round past the belfry at 10:15. He thought nothing of the little bit of bell ringing and shouting at midnight and was astonished to hear the next morning that the wooden bell tower had burned to the ground. Lucas, a tutor, said he'd seen fireballs tossed at the belfry and heard shouts for Fremont and other candidates.

Sunday morning the entire village went to see what had happened in the night. Ben, Ellen, and Johnnie walked into the deep campus and could smell the disaster before they saw it. Ashes, the belfry was ashes. The blackened mound of the college bell lay on its side in the gray dust.

Chapter Twenty-One

Chapel Hill
October 1, 1856

Ben paced the floor of his six-sided room. Today's *Standard* lay open on his desk, the headline blaring "Fremont in the South." Holden had printed the letter under the brave signature "Alumnus." Ben met himself walking to and fro. He was quite beside himself.

This was too much. Was there no more freedom of thought and speech in the state? He knew he would write a reply to "Alumnus" whose identity he deduced - Earnhardt - even though he questioned whether the ridiculous accusations deserved a reply.

The tall oaks on the lawn might save themselves the trouble of trying to soothe his spirit. There was much bad feeling and confusion in the air even here in Chapel Hill. He remembered the scene in the post office when he'd been accosted. Maybe he himself was like a lightning rod attracting the force of those who were furious when anyone breathed opposition to their sacred slaveholding.

He flung himself down into the new desk chair Ellen was so proud of. What was the answer? He had heard of no way to end slavery suddenly without chaos. But because it existed was no reason to extend its very questionable benefits and certain evils into new states.

It was all so ridiculous - the terrible thing I, Benjamin, had said on Primary Day. And because I cannot with integrity retract what I said, I am labeled a hothead. The Governor must understand what I feel, but he insists I just let it pass. Can I really stand against the man who has been my true supporter? It will be the hardest thing I've ever had to do. Doesn't he know "What does it profit a man to gain the world if he loses his own soul?"

He found he was pacing again. In the other room he heard Johnnie shout and Ellen shush him. So much love.

Governor Swain has been the instrument of my salvation, so far, carrying me into this new level of life for myself and my family; first the *Almanac* and Harvard, then to the professorship here. I feel a lump in my throat thinking of how much I love my work here. Dare I oppose the Governor's counsel? This time I must. If I am to have the respect of myself, I must send ol' Holden a reply to the smear on my character he has printed. Wish I didn't have the feeling that drawing me out is just what he wants. But that can't be helped. It's nothing compared to the absolute certainty I have that I must do this. I will have no peace until I answer this charge.

He stopped pacing and smiled at the notion that he was in good company, not wanting to do what he must do. There was Moses and there was Jeremiah the prophet who thought he was too young - and, oh, Samuel who tried not to hear. There was a connection. Why did he have to be the one to see through the delusion all around that slavery was a moral good?

Then his grandfather was walking there with him, walking his long farmer's step and telling him that he was right. Holden must have his reply so that the world would know why Professor Hedrick said he would like to see Fremont elected President. Grandfather Sherwood not only agreed that slavery should not be extended but believed it should not exist. He knew men in North Carolina who'd suffered because of going against the slavocracy.

Ben pictured the older man's face the day he and his family left Davidson County for Iowa. Only now did Ben realize what it had meant; his grandfather had been willing to leave the world he knew, where he'd been a founder and officer of the county, for the unknown West because he wanted to live in a free place.

But isn't North Carolina part of a free country, the United States of America? Isn't our country free? Great-great Grandfather Peter Hedrick from the Palatinate in Germany fought for the United States to be free. The great Judge Gaston said right here in Chapel Hill that slavery is a great evil and must be removed. Surely I can't be wrong to restate what he said twenty years ago. I might even be of some influence if I can write a reasonable letter. And I won't come out flatly against slavery; I'll be that prudent. Just against the extension of it.

He felt lighter to remember that Ellen approved of his writing an answer. Then he sat down at his desk, pulled the lamp over closer, and began to write.

Messrs. Editor:

In the last "Standard" I see a communication signed "Alumnus." Although my name in not mentioned, it was evidently intended for me. Now, politics not being my trade, I feel some hesitation appearing before the public, especially at a time like this when there seems to be a greater desire to stir up strife and hatred than to cultivate feelings of respect and kindness. But, lest my silence be misinterpreted, I will reply to this, it appears to me, uncalled for attack on my politics.

Then, to make the matter short, I say I am in favor of the election of Fremont to the Presidency, and these are the reasons for my preference.

1st. Because I like the man. He was born and educated at the South. He has lived at the North and the West and therefore has an advantage not possessed by his competitors. He is known and honored both at home and abroad. He has shown his love of country by unwavering devotion to its interests. And whether teaching school for the support of his widowed mother, or exploring the wilds of the great West, whether enlarging the boundaries of science or acquiring for our country the Golden State, whether establishing that state's constitution or occupying a seat in the Senate of the nation - in every position and under all circumstances, he has always possessed the courage to undertake and the wisdom to carry through.

In reference to the value of his services in California, Mr. Buchanan says, "He bore a conspicuous part in the conquest of California, and in my opinion is better entitled to be called the conqueror of California than any other man." For such services and abilities I love to do him honor. Platforms and principles are good enough in their places, but for the Presidential chair, the first requisite is the man.

2nd. Because Fremont is on the right side of the great question which now disturbs the public peace. Opposition to slavery extension is neither a Northern nor a Southern sectionalism. It originated with the great Southern statesmen of the Revolution. Washington, Jefferson, Patrick Henry, Madison, and Randolph were all opposed to slavery in the abstract, and were all opposed *to admitting it into new territory. One of the early acts of the patriots of the Revolution was to pass the ordinance of '87 by which slavery was excluded from all the territories we then possessed. Many of these great men were slave-holders, but they did not let self-interest blind them to the evils of the system.*

Jefferson said that slavery exerts an evil influence on both the whites and the blacks, but that he was opposed to the abolition of slavery by which slaves would be turned loose among whites. In his autobiography he says....

Ben went to a book shelf and located the familiar book, sat down, found the page he'd marked and continued to write.

"Nothing is more certainly written in the book of fate, than that these people are to be free, nor is it less certain that the two races, equally free, cannot live in the same government. Nature, habit, opinion, have drawn indelible lines between them."

Among the evils which he says slavery brings on whites is to make them tyrannical and idle. "With the morals of the people their industry is also destroyed. For in a warm climate no man will labor for himself who can make another labor for him. This is true: of the proprietors of slaves a very small population indeed are ever seen to labor."

What was true in Jefferson's time is true now. I might go on and on and give "Alumnus" every week from now to the election, a column of good "Black Republican" documents all written by the most eminent Southern statesmen beginning with Washington and including nearly all of eminence for ability, virtue, and patriotism down to our times. No later than 1850, Henry Clay declared in the Senate, "I cannot and never will vote, and no earthly power can make me vote to spread slavery over territory where it does not exist." While opposed to slavery, he was, like Fremont, opposed to the least interference by the general government where it does exist.

Should there be any with subjects belonging to state policy, either by other States or by the federal government, no one would be more ready than myself to defend the "good old North," my native State. But with Washington, Jefferson, Franklin, Henry, Randolph, Clay, and Webster for political teachers, I cannot believe that slavery extension is one of the constitutional rights of the South. If "Alumnus" thinks that Calhoun was a wiser statesman or better Southerner than either Washington or Jefferson, he is welcome to his opinion. I shall not attempt to abridge his liberty in the least. But my own opinions I will have, whether he is willing to grant me that as a free man or not. I believe I have had quite as good an opportunity as he has to form an opinion on the questions now to be settled. And when "Alumnus" talks of driving me out for sentiments once held by these great men, I cannot help thinking he is becoming rather a fanatical.

For the information of "Alumnus" I will state that he has put himself to unnecessary trouble in blazoning this matter before the public. The whole matter belongs exclusively to the jurisdiction of the Trustees of the University. They are men of integrity and influence, and have at heart the best interest of the University. There is no difficulty in bringing this or any other question relating to Faculty or students before them.

"Alumnus" has also made another mistake in supposing the Faculty take on themselves influencing the political opinions of the students. The students come to college, generally, with their policies already fixed, and it is exceedingly rare for them to change while here. I have been connected with our University, as student and

Professor, for six years, and am free to say that I know no institution, North or South, from which partisan politics and sectarian religion are so entirely excluded. And yet we are often attacked by bigots of both.

For my own part, I do not know the politics of more than one in a hundred of the students, except that I might infer it from knowing the politics of their fathers. And they would not have known of my predilections in the present contest had not one of them asked me which one of the candidates I preferred.

But if "Alumnus" would understand that state of things here correctly, he had better make a visit to the University. He would find each member of the Faculty busy teaching in his own department, whether science or literature, and that party politics is one of the branches which we leave to the student to study at home at some other place or time.

If "Alumnus" does conclude to visit us, there is another matter to which I might direct his attention. The two societies here, to the one or the other of which all students belong, each have a very good library, and in those libraries are to be found the "complete works" of our great statesmen.

Now for fears the minds of the students might be "poisoned" by reading some of these staunch old patriots, would it be well for "Alumnus" to exert himself, through Legislature or otherwise to drive them out of the libraries? It is true that the works of Calhoun are in the same case with those of Jefferson, but from appearances, the Virginian seems to be read pretty often whilst the South Carolinian maintains a posture of "masterly inactivity."

When I was a student in College a few years ago, the young politicians used to debate in the halls of the societies the same questions which the old politicians were debating in the Halls of Congress. The side which opposed slavery in the abstract generally had the books in their favor, and they quite often had "the best of the argument." So that when Col. Fremont said that he was "Opposed to slavery in the abstract and upon principle, sustained and made habitual by long-settled convictions," he but uttered the sentiments of the best Southern people from the Revolution down to the present day, and, may I add, of the majority of the people among whom I was born and educated.

Of my neighbors, friends, and kindred, nearly half have left the state since I was old enough to remember.

Many is the time I have stood by the loaded emigrant wagon and given the parting hand to those whose face I was never to look upon again. They were going to seek homes in the free West, knowing as they did, that free and slave labor could not both exist and prosper at the same community.

If anyone thinks that I speak without knowledge, let him refer to the last census. He will find that in 1850 there were 58,000 native North Carolinians living in the free States of the West. 31,000 in Indiana alone. There were at the same time 180,000 Virginians living in the free states. Now if these people were so much in love with the "institution," why did they not remain where they could enjoy its blessing?

It is not, however, my object to attack the institution of slavery. But even the most zealous defender of the patriarchal institution cannot shut his eyes to a few facts. One is that in nearly all the slave States, there is a deficiency of labor. Since the abolition of the African slave trade, there is no source of obtaining a supply except from natural increase. For this reason, among others, a gentleman from South Carolina, in an article in Debow's Review, for August, 1856, advocates a dissolution of the Union in order that the African slave trade may be revived.

From North Carolina and Virginia nearly the entire increase of the slave population during the last twenty years has been sent off to the new States in the Southwest. In my boyhood I lived on one of the great thoroughfares (near Lock's Bridge on the Yadkin River) and have seen as many as 2,000 in a single day going South, mostly in the hands of speculators.

Now the loss of these 2,000 did the State a greater injury than would the shipping off of a million dollars. I think I may ask any sensible man how we are to grow rich and prosper while driving out a million dollars a day? I am glad, however, to say that the ruinous policy is not now carried on to such an extent as it has been. But there is still too much of it.

I have very little doubt that if the slaves which are now scattered thinly over Tennessee, Kentucky, and Missouri were back in Virginia and North Carolina, it would be better for all concerned. These old states could then go on and develop the immense wealth which must remain locked for many years to come. Whilst the new States, free from a system which degrades white labor would become a land of Common Schools, thrift, and industry - equal if not superior to any in the Union. But letting that be as it may, still no one can deny that here in North Carolina we need more men, rather than more land. Then why go to war to make more slave States when we have too much territory already for the force we have to work with?

Our fathers fought for freedom and one of the tyrannical acts which they threw in the teeth of Great Britain was that she forced slaves upon the colonies against their will. Now the secessionists are trying to dissolve the Union because they are not permitted to establish slavery in the Territory of Kansas. If the institution of slavery is a good and desirable thing in itself, it is the easiest thing in the world for the people to vote for its introduction at any time after they have formed a Constitution and been admitted as a State. If it is not a thing good and desirable, it would be an act of great oppression to force it upon them. For, however anyone may lament the evils of slavery, it is almost impossible to get rid of the system when once introduced. Nullify it by law if you will; the evil remains, possibly aggravated. But in the new State, a few words in the Constitution may prevent the entire evil from entering.

From my knowledge of the people of North Carolina, I believe the majority who will go to Kansas during the next five years would prefer it to be as a free state. I am sure that if I would go there I would vote to exclude slavery. In doing so, I believe that I should advance the best interests of Kansas and, at the same time, benefit North Carolina and Virginia by preventing the carrying away of slaves who may be more profitably employed at home.

Born in the "good old North State," I cherish a love for her and her people that I bear no other state or people. It will ever be my sincere wish to advance her interests. I love also the Union of the States, secured as it was by the blood of my ancestors, and whatever influence I possess, small though it may be, shall be exerted for its preservation.

I do not claim infallibility for my opinions. Wiser and better men have been mistaken. But holding as I do the doctrines once advocated by Washington and Jefferson, I think I should be met by argument, not by denunciation. At any rate, those who denounce me should at least support their charges by their own names.

He shook his weary hand and worked his cramped fingers. Then he signed, "B.S. Hedrick, Chapel Hill, October 1, 1856."

Opening the door into the hallways, he yelled, "Ellen!" while rushing toward the parlor. She met him at the doorway and was engulfed by his hard embrace.

She knew it was done. He was an exhausted man.

Later that night when she had read the letter, she gave him full support. "You had to do this, Benjamin, my love, and you've done it well."

"That means everything, honey; we're together on this, aren't we?"

"Yes, we are together, whatever comes of it. But Ben," she ventured, "don't you think it might be a little too long? I mean, maybe more people would read your side of it if it was a little shorter."

"I know, I had that feeling too, Ellen, but maybe I'm too tired to see how to cut it down. Could you show me where you think I could trim it?"

After a half hour or so of toiling over the document, Ellen said, "No, everything you've written needs to be said. I say it has to be as it is."

And so the fateful letter was mailed the next morning.

Chapter Twenty-Two

Chapel Hill
October 4-11, 1856

Benjamin's letter, headlined "The Defence" was printed by a gleeful Editor Holden on Saturday, October 4. The chosen victim had stepped into the trap, and the hunters closed in immediately.

In the study Saturday night, Ben and Ellen mulled matters over and stared at the accomplished fact. "The Defence" could hardly be overlooked since it filled the front page of the *Standard*. The defendant was feeling both relieved to be in print and apprehensive about what might happen. He was accepting large doses of praise from his chief supporter when strange sounds were heard from the direction of the campus.

The sounds continued from that direction; it was a small uproar of some kind. It reminded Ben of something he'd heard before...oh, it sounded a lot like this time last year when the students had burned ol' Charlie in effigy.

Ellen joined his lookout and agreed. "Let's go back inside," she suggested before either voiced the possibility that this uproar, not a very large one from the sound of it, might be Ben's turn at being roasted.

Both were relieved when Charles Phillips came down Franklin and up their long lawn to give them the news. Ben didn't know whether his colleague was being kind or vengeful as a news bearer but was glad he came anyway.

"Thought you'd want to know," Phillips said when he'd taken a chair in the parlor. "We heard a gathering on campus, so I went upstairs to look out. You got a bigger crowd than I did last year, I'm glad to say- glad, that is, for me, not you."

His face was pinker than usual. "Still, not many. Maybe fifty or so, and yes, somebody got up an effigy, not much of a resemblance, they named you. Made its face black, of course. They lit it just as I looked out. That was when the loudest cheer went up. You could hear it from here, couldn't you?"

"Yes, we could," Ben answered. He felt somewhere inside, an increased wariness of the blustery man. "Then what?"

"Well, the thing burned up and the crowd broke up. Not much to it really. This kind of thing fades quickly if no attention is paid." He was thinking the boy was still not properly contrite.

"If only you hadn't sent that thing in to Holden!" he blurted, and looked down at Ben with an expression that mingled exasperation and pity.

Sunday was Ellen's birthday and obligingly dawned bright and clear. As usual, Ben and Ellen left the little boys with Melie and walked up Franklin to the Presbyterian Church. Both were conscious of a new deliberateness in holding their heads high. Not that they were proud, just so no one could think they were ashamed.

As they passed the front of the campus, neither stole so much as a glance toward the scene of last night's ruckus. The town was used to student cut-ups, yet all the same, the angle of the head seemed newly important.

Everyone was walking to church today. Gentlemen lifted top hats, ladies nodded bonnets, ruffled or feathered. Along with the Presbyterians came the Methodists and Baptists. The Episcopalians were out of sight on the other end of Franklin. Of course those living too far away -poor things- came in carriages or buggies to raise a dust which settled impartially on the church-goers of Chapel Hill.

Arriving at the small white church with the Hedricks were the Mitchells. Mrs. Mitchell's nod was definitely briefer than usual, Ellen noted. The two couples entered the little church and sat in their customary pews. Nothing in the atmosphere seemed to indicate shock or revulsion.

Not so across the street in the college campus. President Swain was addressing the students about the problem of Professor Hedrick's article in the *Standard*. That is, he was assuring them that all was well. And they were not to be disturbed; the college was taking steps to see that the right thing was done. He chastised them mildly about the demonstration Saturday night, but not so much as to arouse the envy of those who hadn't taken part.

To his satisfaction, Swain noticed the usual indifference of most of the students while he was speaking. In this instance he would have been glad it some had dozed off, as had happened in the past. No reason they should be excited. Sometimes he wondered why he cared so much about these young fellows, but he did, and he would protect them from dangerous ideas and protect the institution against the withdrawal of slave-holders' sons. What in the world would happen if such a thing got started? David Swain, former governor of the state and current president of the University, knew exactly what he was doing, much as he regretted what might happen to the young man he had regarded almost as a son.

After Sunday dinner and a nap at his home in Raleigh, former governor Charles Manley, now secretary of the Executive Committee of the Board of Trustees, got right to it. He wrote Governor Swain at Chapel Hill, as well as he could with his hands shaking so.
"Professor Hedrick's political essay which appeared in yesterday's *Standard* gave great pain to the trustees and friends of the University. The Committee had already met," he wrote," and voted to fire the professor, but the motion was withdrawn in favor of having Swain

persuade him to resign. Their reason was they wished to avoid seeing a martyr get too much attention in the North."

Governor Swain responded by calling a meeting of the faculty at noon on Monday, October 6. It was at this meeting that Ben realized he was in serious trouble in regard to his beloved position as professor. He also realized, as he hadn't before, the depth of his colleagues' bondage to the status quo.

The President told the assembled faculty he had convened them to consider the publication of Professor Hedrick in the *North Carolina Standard* of Saturday.

Ben shifted in his chair and, with an effort, held his head up; he was looking into the eyes of Charles Phillips who sat across from him. Phillips did not meet his glance. Later Ben reflected it was at this moment that he knew his fate was sealed.

But for now he was listening to the Governor and steeling himself to take one moment at a time and not to give an inch.

Ol' Warping Bars was holding forth on the necessity of keeping political matters strictly out of the college. He agreed with that part of the "Defence" stating that this separation was adhered to at the University; he elaborated that this was necessary for the reputation, prosperity, and usefulness of the University. He noted that even sermons in the college chapel had been restricted to the leading doctrines of Christianity in which no differences exist among us.

Ben made a quick connection in his mind to the recent Archbishop flap and knew the Governor had been profoundly grateful the prelate had declined the student's unauthorized invitation to speak at the University. More than one issue was closed to freedom.

Swain was going on that another reason for this no politics policy was respect for the different tenets and opinions of those present.

But that doesn't include my tenets and opinions, Ben thought. It was a long meeting for him. He knew his face was flushed, his forehead beaded with sweat, his hair divided into tight damp curls. The room, which had been full of friends and colleagues, was now an enemy camp in which he played David to an invincible Goliath. And Ben felt that Yahweh was pretty far away at the moment.

Out of the tension, Elisha Mitchell spoke, asking that a committee be appointed to consider the President's communication.

Professors Mitchell, Phillips, and Hubbard became the committee and withdrew to draw up resolutions.

While the men were out, the meeting recessed, and Ben and Henri Harrissee stepped outside together. Ben knew the French professor was also in hot water- in his case, for poor discipline in his classes. Henri placed his hand on Ben's sleeve.

"Benjamin, I am proud of you. Never mind what happens here, you have done a good and a right thing."

"Thank you, Henri. The Lord knows I need somebody to see what I tried to do."

"Oui. I'm just sorry I can't be of more use to you. But you know they are out for my scalp. Probably, it is better if I don't say anything. But I can't promise. Look at it this way; there are other places which wouldn't be so hemmed in as this little country college."

Ben laughed and felt better. The ringing in his ears stopped. "You are right, Henri, you might do me a favor by keeping your support just between you and me. I'm just a North Carolina country boy who's had a taste of life at the North but still knows where home is."

"Ah, Benjamin, who knows what will happen to either of us?" He shrugged his shoulders and held out his hands in his Gallic way.

The two men strolled to the end of the walkway in front of South Building and now retraced their steps slowly, silently.

When they returned to the meeting room, the others were all seated and they looked at Ben accusingly. The quiet was eloquent. Proceedings resumed with the reading of the committee's resolutions, in the deep voice of Professor Mitchell.

Resolved, that the course pursued by Professor Hedrick as set forth in his publication in the North Carolina Standard is not warranted by our usage;

and the political opinions expressed are not those entertained by any other member of this body.

Resolved, that while we feel duty bound to declare our sentiments freely upon this occasion, we entertain none other than feelings of personal respect and kindness for the subject of them; and sincerely regret the indiscretion into which he seems in this instance to have fallen.

They had gone along with Swain's condemnation, as Ben felt was sure to happen. He felt it in his gut. There were murmurs of approval, and then the call for a vote. President Swain called the name of each faculty member, and with one exception, all voted to accept the resolutions.

At home, Ellen saw Ben's face and knew he'd been shaken. As he described the meeting, she wept a little before getting control of herself for his sake. "What shall we do?" was her staunch response, meaning we are in this together, and there is something we can do.

"I don't know. Write Governor Bragg maybe..." He hated to see her cry, yet envied her the freedom to release her feelings.

"Yes, he's the Chairman of the Board of Trustees, isn't he?" She sniffed and went on. "Maybe you should just explain the whole thing, as you see it. He's probably heard King Billy's more than once......" She wiped her nose with her lace-edged handkerchief.

"Father, Father," Johnnie called as he whirled into the room. "Look at all the gum balls Melie and me found!" He held up his small basket with a few of the prickly spheres in the bottom.

Ben stooped to the level of his bright-eyed son and admired the balls. "Tell you what, John ol' boy, let's go out and find enough to fill this basket!"

Johnnie was pulling at his hand as soon as the suggestion was made. Ben looked back at Ellen with a warm feeling of thankfulness and security. "I'll get to the letter tonight."

After writing a lengthy letter to Governor Manley Monday night, Ben had the feeling he had done all he could do on his own behalf. He reread the last paragraph:

> *"I have no means of knowing in what light this matter will be viewed by the Trustees. But as it is an important one, to me at least, I hope they will give it careful consideration before coming to a decision. I cannot see that my letter to the Standard involves in any way the opinions of other members of the faculty, at least it should not."*

He still had a hard knot of self-justification inside, the knowing that "The Defence" was something he had to do for his integrity and that what followed was out of his hands.

There was consolation in having a broader view than most of the villagers, of knowing there was support for his opposition to the extension of slavery- support in many places. Besides those quiet persons in the Carolinas who felt that way, he suspected there were thousands in the North- such as most of their Cambridge friends-and out west such as dear old Grandfather Sherwood. Most of those were just out-and-out against slavery-abolitionists. Maybe he was leaning that way too, but he knew enough about local feelings not to say that. Abolitionist was a fighting word. But now it seemed that his mild dissent from the way Southerners were supposed to think was just as bad. And he could hear Governor Swain saying, "I told you so."

Ben hadn't even told Ellen how hurt he had been to hear the boys had burned him in effigy. Up 'til now, he'd been very pleased at the respect the students had shown him, because after all, he was not much older than some of them. He'd felt he had their regard both as a person and as a professor. Youth was fickle, easily whipped in the wind of whatever blew past. The crowd's fun had wounded him. Ellen shared his feelings so deeply, he hadn't wanted to add to her pain.

Governor Swain felt he was in command of a battle, that he must keep up with several outposts at a time. One of his prime strategies was keeping communication open to the Trustees Executive Committee. That meant much correspondence with Charles Manley, the Committee secretary. Swain sat down Monday morning long enough to pour out his concerns and thus, he hoped share the responsibility.

> "Hedrick has the courage of a lion and the obstinacy of a mule. He can neither be frightened, coaxed, or persuaded in anything. He consulted me as to the propriety of replying to Alumnus, and entered into the contest in opposition to the most determined opposition. He communicated his determination to reply and exhibited his reply itself to no one but his wife. He will sit in
>
> His tracks without moving a muscle, and I am not sure he does not covet the crown of martyrdom...
>
> If you award the crown of martyrdom immediately, and Col. Fremont succeeds in the election, you make his fortune. He understands this too well to think for a moment of resignation.
>
> Sparing him at present will give Freesoilers new strength in the South, while the charge of persecution for opinion's sake, will add to the tempest which is sweeping over the nation. If you proceed to extremes at once, I would avoid a political issue, and second the action taken by the faculty and approved by the Trustees in the Archbishop

case- a violation of the usages of the institution, not as a
Freesoiler but as a partisan."

But David Swain had doubts as well as regrets about what
the Executive Committee seemed ready to do. Did that small group
have the legal right to fire a professor? Honesty sat him down to write
Manley again that same day.

> "If there were not much better lawyers, members
> of the Executive Committee than I am, I might be tempted
> to enter upon an analysis of the Charter and subsequent
> acts of the General Assembly to show that the Committee
> has no power to remove a professor."

He proceeded with the analysis anyway and then continued
to suggest what the Committee ought to do if it did decide it had the
power to remove a professor.

> "It seems to me the exercise of it may be forborne
> for many reasons when the annual meeting of the Board is
> so near at hand. Be advised that a committee conduct an
> investigation on the scene and that this would strengthen
> its hand."(5)

The general was calling in his troops. Attacks were coming from all sides. He wrote:

> "...a professor must be removed not arbitrarily or capriciously for mere difference of opinion in religion or politics which the Committee may seem sufficient. But for misbehavior, inability, or neglect of duty. Hedrick may very properly be arraigned for departing from our established usages, and this should be the only count in the impeachment." (6)

President Swain had done all he could.

With an inner defensiveness he hoped didn't show, Ben went through the long week of meeting classes, conducting laboratory tests, lecturing, and walking to and from Smith Building in campus traffic—all this in the new spotlight he felt picking him out.

He sensed reluctance in students' greeting; some would not meet his eyes.

When Saturday's *Standard* arrived, another blow fell. Holden had published the faculty resolutions along with his own piercing rejoinder:

> "Nothing remains now but to cut off, if it should

be necessary, the offending member. Mr. Hedrick, it seems,

was present at the meeting of the Faculty on the 6ᵗʰ; and

it is not stated that he withdrew from the meeting. Almost

anyone, it seems to us, would have resigned at once; but

either he does not appreciate the delicacy of his situation,

or he is waiting to be dismissed so he may become a lion

at Cambridge, or some other black Republican circle. It is

obvious that his usefulness as a professor in our University

is gone; and the sooner he leaves, or is discharged from it,

the better for the institution itself and for the character of

the state."

He went on to disclaim any connection with the effigy burning, and to remind readers that their editor had charged Hedrick with treason to his section and to the Constitution. He scoffed at the arguments of the "Defence" as unworthy of a response because "we do not choose to argue with a black Republican." He concluded the lengthy diatribe cautioning the students not to think he is lecturing them, to leave the professor alone because the Executive Committee [as he well knew] would do its duty and wipe the stain away, restoring "peace and good feeling."

News came to Chapel Hill, to both the hunted and the hunters, of rising indignation in the state at the "Defence" and its author. In Raleigh, Holden felt something of the satisfaction of a composer conducting his own work, since none of his fellow editors had dared to reprint the offending article.

Among the satisfying news were resolutions from a citizens' meeting in the far eastern (read wealthy slave-holding county) North Carolina town of Murfreesboro: "we the citizens of Hertford County, in N.C, having some education at the University, feeling a deep interest in all that pertains to its welfare, feel it to be our duty to express our opinions in regard to the course of said Hedrick and of promptly denouncing same."

After this difficult week of working on campus, Ben felt the letter Holden published on the 11th was heaping more earth on his grave, though he wouldn't have said this to anyone. The letter was another anonymous one, though many judged it to come from Clingman, a trustee from the mountains. The writer read "with astonishment and regret that a man who calls himself a Professor of the university should so undervalue the interest of that institution as to advertise himself the advocate of the sentiments he avowed."

"Anonymous" was clearly a lawyer, his speech betrayed him. He went on to state his confidence in the noble Board of Trustees, sixty gentlemen dispersed all over the state. He knew duty would be done, and he, in advance, repudiated the man he wouldn't dignify with the appellation of Professor.

The "traitorous" professor found it hard to believe himself the subject of such fiery rhetoric. He was sweating in the limelight that played on him with each issue of the Raleigh paper. But he got some satisfaction in Governor Swain's continued friendliness. When the Governor met Ben on the campus, he was as quick with his slanted grin as ever. If either had changed in the relationship, to all appearances, it was Ben.

He felt a certain embarrassment in the company of his mentor since he now found himself in straits after going against his advice. He was loathe to seem the beggar in the presence of the king, and actually didn't feel so much the beggar as perhaps a knight who was about to go on a long journey to another country. He smiled to himself at the fanciful notion.

And then he acknowledged certain exhilaration. Was it release from bondage? Funny, he'd had no realization until recently that he was in any kind of bondage. The question hadn't come up. He had been free to do what he wanted, had been given help to gain a good position in life, one in which he could support Ellen and the children. But it was by his own hand and steady work that he had been able to reach and keep that position.

If now, following the urges of his inner being, he was to move on, so be it. He felt both fear and excitement. Then he admonished himself that he was getting ahead of the process. He wasn't planning to leave this college unless he was forced.

Just now he was walking up the slope to home. High in the oaks, a squirrel leapt from one branch to another, rode the swaying branch to safety. Ben inwardly applauded the feat of strength and balance. Maybe he could learn something from the little gray creature.

Chapter Twenty-Three

Chapel Hill
October 12, 1856

After church services were over, Ben and Ellen stopped outside to chat with the Mitchells. Dr. Mitchell asked Ben, "Are you going over to Raleigh to the Fair this week?" His face seemed as benign as ever.

"Yes," Ben answered, "I plan to go. Really I feel I have to—the *Cultavator*, you know, we've been pushing farmers to enter the exhibits, guess I'd better turn up to see what comes in and what wins the prizes."

"Certainly, I can see that, thought you'd be going."
Ellen and Mrs. Mitchell exchanged smiles and listened.

"Well listen, Benjamin," Mitchell continued, "while you're in Raleigh you might hear about the Southern Governors meeting. Hear they're 'sposed to meet to talk about what to do if a...," he lowered his voice and rolled his eyes, "a Republican should win for president."

He means well, Ben thought, and said, "Don't know a thing about that, Professor Mitchell. Politics is new to me, you know."

After dinner the family enjoyed the sunny afternoon. Beside the front steps Johnnie helped his baby brother put acorns in a box but found it hard work since Charlie thought it more fun to turn them out on the ground. Over and over, the filling and the dumping went on. Their parents laughed quietly from the seats on the porch.

"He surprised you, didn't he?" Ellen asked Ben.

"You mean Dr. Mitchell and the Fair, don't you?"

"Yes, had you forgotten about it? Do you think you ought to go?"

"Honey, you know I've had other things on my mind~that Trustee's letter in the paper yesterday! But I made plans weeks ago for Charlie Phillips to supervise lab that day. Hadn't really thought much more about it. Why shouldn't I go?"

"You know what I mean~this trouble. I feel like a lot of people~ more than we thought~are upset about your letter. They read it like a threat. You don't suppose they'd do you any harm, do you, my darling?" She raised her eyebrows in question and placed her warm palm over the back of his hand.

"Don't worry, sugar, what could happen at the good ol' annual Fair?" He looked at his beautiful anxious wife. "I'm so thankful for you, sweetheart. Even more now that it seems like things are shaking around us."

Her eyes filled as they kissed. Baby Charlie's scream ended that. He lay flat on his back in a rug of acorns where his exasperated brother had pushed him before running off down the lawn.

October 14

Ellen nodded off as she waited up for Ben beside the flickering lamp in the parlor. His step on the porch startled her, then brought a warm flooding sense of relief. He was home. Thank you, Lord.

After he'd told her about the Fair, about seeing her Pa, Henry and Selina there, and about visiting the courteous Governor Manly, his blue eyes began to twinkle the way they did when he was about to come out with something funny. "I haven't told you the big news yet," he said unable to suppress a smile.

She snuggled up under his arm and murmured, not too concerned, "And what might that be?"

"Well, the Southern Governors meeting yesterday was not a rousing success. I heard several versions of the story but all agreed Governor Wise of Virginia had done the inviting of all the governors of Southern states. Wanted to get them to push for secession if Fremont wins. Trouble was, the rascals didn't come. Just Wise and Adams from South Carolina~and of course Governor Bragg was host."

"H'm'm, sounds like most southern states aren't that worked up about the Republicans. Maybe the Trustees will take heart~or have a heart and not think you're so dangerous after all."

"Maybe. Of course King Billy Holden was in on the meeting, too, along with some other big Democrats like Clingman~bet you anything he wrote that nasty Trustee letter. But anyway, the governors and friends un-met in a hurry when Holden told them there was talk of getting up a crowd in Raleigh to protest the notion of secession. Anyway, folks at the Fair were getting a big laugh about the whole thing."

"That makes me feel better. Maybe there's still some common sense around after all. But what about you, darling? Did you hear anything about the "Defence? "

"I don't think most of 'em even read it. I felt welcome, enjoyed it, even met a few *Cultivator* readers. Let's go to bed."

October 20, 1856

David Swain snatched up the envelope from Governor Manly as soon as Dr. November brought in the day's mail. First he read it quickly, then he reread, his feelings riding fast head-to-head with his reason. They had done it then. He was both relieved and sad, a painful state of war within.

First he read Manly's letter.

Raleigh,
Oct. 18, 1856

My dear Governor,
I send you herewith a copy of Minutes of the Executive Committee of this day.
As to Hedrick, he is beheaded. I read your letter to the Committee on their power to dismiss. But to no purpose. The "outside pressure" was too great. Please

notify Mr. Hedrick of the decision.

Yours Truly,

Charles Manly

They'd caved in, then, despite his warning that they had no legal right to dismiss a professor, the right resting with the whole Board. He read the report of the meeting, picturing the elderly Manly, the blunt Gov. Bragg, an outraged Col. Steele, a vituperative Saunders.

Whereas, Professor B.S. Hedrick seems disposed to respect neither the opinions of the Faculty nor the Trustees of the University but persists in retaining his situation to the manifest injury of the University.

Resolved, That for the causes set forth by this Committee on the 11 inst., he, the said Benj. S. Hedrick, be and is hereby dismissed as a Professor in the University and the Professorship, which he now fills, is hereby declared to be vacant.

Resolved, That he be paid his full salary to the close of the present session.

Resolved, That the Secretary notify him of this decision.

Committee adjourned.

What would be the kindest way of letting Hedrick know the fruit of his folly? Should he go out to the house later today after classes and tell them together? He pictured pretty Ellen's distress and tears and decided against that. He just might join her weeping.

No, he would send word over to Hedrick's lab that he should come to the President's office as soon as class was dismissed. That should put him here a little after noon.

He scribbled a note in his all but illegible script, which most faculty members learned to make out, with some trouble. Then he called Dr. November and sent him off. He wondered briefly if the aging black man had any idea the forces that swirled around the existence of his race in these parts.

President Swain usually kept his office door open, seemed more hospitable. Thus he heard the poor fellow come into the hallway and approach. He was walking fast, said the creaking floorboards, but he would walk out slowly.

There he was, short little man, but not bad-looking, more like a born gentleman than a farmer's son. "Come on in, Benjamin, and sit down, I need to talk to you."

Ben knew when he walked in the news wasn't good; Ol' Warping Bars' temple vein was leaping a mile a minute. Oh God, why did I do it? I did what seemed right and I am going to be put out, what in the world will I do to make a living? The beautiful golden cast of the fall-blooming campus outside the window was a lie.

Meanwhile, Warping Bars was clearing his throat a few times and telling himself to be kind, this was one of his student-sons after all, even if he had gone astray. "Benjamin, I think you know that you have long been one of my favorites, even though your recent course of action was taken against my advice."

Ben was well aware of that fact and hoped the Governor would get on with it. He could take it. At least he hoped he could. "Yes, Governor Swain, you have been another father to me, and I know you don't wish me any harm."

Swain was relieved. He was going to be sensible about this, now that it was too late. "I have here the proceedings of the meeting of the Executive Committee of the Board of Trustees, and I am to notify you that..." He was having trouble getting it out and had to look away so that Benjamin wouldn't see the tears.

"Here, you can read it for yourself." And he handed him the paper containing the end of his present way of life.

Ben wondered if his face was as red as it felt. His heart was pounding as if to escape his chest. This was it. They had fired him. His position was "now vacant."

"May I show this to Ellen, Governor? I'll return it after she's read it."

Both men stood. They let each other see tears, then they embraced, and Ben went out without another word.

Chapter Twenty-Four

Salisbury, N.C.
October 21, 1856

In July when he was invited to the state Education Convention, Ben hadn't imagined his University position would be ended when October 21 arrived. But since Governor Swain has approved his representing the University at the meeting, he dutifully departed Orange County for Rowan County, some eighty miles to the southwest.

He sincerely wanted to be present in support of Calvin Wiley, recipient of an honorary degree at the University's Commencement in June. Wiley was making a wonderful effort to build the effective school system so badly needed in North Carolina.

Ben had something of a paternal feeling himself toward the delegates who would come, mostly from elementary schools over the state. Ellen said she thought it would do him good to have something else on his mind. And the Rankins, the old friends and mentors of both Hedricks, had invited him to stay with them at their Academy.

He left Chapel Hill Monday afternoon, the 20th, and was now on the train leaving Greensboro. Long knives of sunlight sliced through the dusty windows of the passenger car and the wooden backs of the seats in front of him. He was coming home to Salisbury, the big city of his childhood. His mother came to his mind's eye. She'd loved those rare trips to town; he could remember her smile as she told the children to get ready to go. How amazed she would be to see him now riding on a train through Guilford County, then Davidson (theirs), and on to Rowan and Salisbury.

Just this past January the newspapers had reported the big celebration in Salisbury when the North Carolina Railroad finally completed the connection between Richmond and Charlotte, and on down to Charleston. Now the South was connected by rail to the North, though disconnected in so many other ways.

Mother would be stunned all right, even though she'd been a forward-looking person. What a gift to have had an educated mother before there were any schools to speak of in their neighborhood. It was beside her soft warm person that he first grasped the meaning of letters. Some afternoons she'd taken time from working the garden to cultivate her oldest offshoot. She was so eager for her children to share the treasure of reading.

"You're smart, Bennie," she said more than once. "You're going to be somebody," she said and gave him a tender look to go with the encouraging words.

What would she think of him now? He doubted that this notoriety he now seemed to have would fit into her notion of being somebody.

He knew a little sob, deep inside, far too deep to get out, he hoped. Ma was really proud the day he read the first line of Genesis to her. Even now "In the beginning God..." went with the sound of string beans snapping and the sight of Mother's profile with her straight nose and tightly pinned brown hair.

As the car lurched and stopped again--probably another cow on the tracks between the red clay banks--he talked with the ghost he'd evoked. He explained the situation and why he'd gotten into it. "Well, Bennie," she said, looking sorrowful and yearning at the same time, "Seems like you've gotten yourself into a corner, with the help of that editor, but I can see it's for the right. As you say, Father is on your side, and a man has got to speak up for what he believes is right. Things must be bad if there's no more freedom than you say." She patted his hand, and he felt better for their conversation.

The conductor opened the car door and let in some flying cinders and the roar of the engine and the clack of the wheels against the rails. The grating of brakes and lurching of passengers accompanied his shout of "Salisbury".

Ben got to his feet and gathered his traveling bag and brief case, Ellen's gift before they'd left Cambridge, bless her. The dark shape within him had been waiting to rise up and fill his consciousness, and there it was just in time to get off at Salisbury with him. Oh God, why? Be with us and keep us from bitterness at being treated as if

I'd done something unspeakable. He saw his father standing at the edge of the station shed. He respects me, dear old Father. He won't understand, but I'll try my best to make him see.

Ben stepped down from the train after waiting for a fat lady and her little boy to get off first. Might be Mrs. Fisher, but he'd been away so long he wasn't sure. She hadn't known him either, he supposed, since she hadn't spoken. Or did she know him and choose not to speak?

I mustn't start thinking like that. I meant every word~and more~I sent to King Billy.

"Father!" He put his arm around the taller smiling man who'd worn his Sunday suit to meet the son he beamed at proudly. He had aged a bit around the eyes.

"Bennie, I'm glad to see you, son. How'd you like riding our new Iron Horse?"

That was about as effusive as John Leonard Hedrick could be. Ben could tell he'd heard the rumors and was prepared to stick with his boy who'd gone to college and then turned out to be a professor. Ben saw him turn his head to check out who was in the station that he could present the pride of the family to. There were quite a few folks meeting convention delegates who'd come in on the train, quite a little crowd milling about.

"Howdy, George," John spoke to a fellow townsman who'd also

donned his Sunday suit to meet someone. The red-faced man stopped. "George, it's Bennie. You 'member my boy who got so much larnin' at the University, he's a Professor."

George ducked his head slightly but didn't extend his hand. "Listen here, Ben," he said, his brindled mustache wiggling, "folks here are kinda upset 'bout your piece in the Raleigh paper, that is, what the *Banner* said you said. If I was you, I'd lay low. I don't bear you no grudge, mind, it just ain't safe nowadays to say what you said."

"What's wrong, George, isn't this a free country anymore?" Ben had let his anger out more than he'd meant to. Father was pulling his sleeve.

"Come on, Bennie, this is fine you've come early. Let's go over to the house; John will be tickled to death to see you. We got your letter you were coming to the convention, but we didn't really look for you 'til tomorrow."

He was embarrassed, John Hedrick was. After all, he was a prominent local citizen.

Ben wondered what his father really thought about the "Defence," as he let himself be pulled along. They were walking down Ennis Street, and he was ten years old again. The Hedricks were riding in a farm wagon, cleaned up for the occasion. Ma and Father were on the seat with John between them, the rest of the children knocking around in the wagon bed.

Unexpectedly, Ben felt the sting of tears behind his eyelids as his father escorted him protectively, with little glances to each side. How very sad if the slow climb up he had made should quickly crash. Had crashed. Here came Mr. Rankin. He'd want to argue into the night. Made Ben feel tired to see him.

"Why, Benjamin!" the older man exclaimed. "We didn't look for you until tomorrow." His manner was kind as ever but his left eye with the involuntary wink Ben remembered from Classical School was working overtime. Ben assured Mr. Rankin he would stay with his father tonight and come to the Academy after the meeting tomorrow night. "We're proud of this young man, aren't we, Mr. Hedrick?" Mr. Rankin said, pumping John Hedrick's hand.

And father and son left the center of the little town and went into the country to the Hedrick home. The girls were both away at Edgeworth School in Greensboro where Ellen had studied. But young John was at home and delighted by a day in the company of the older brother he admired.

After being with his family, talking his head off about the evident dismissal and what preceded it, and listening in between to all that had happened since they last met, Ben caught himself looking forward to the Convention's opening meeting Tuesday night. Father said he'd go along as a spectator; see if the schools were in good hands.

Father and son mingled with the small crowd heading toward the Presbyterian Church. "Bet Wiley's tickled with this good turnout," said a youngish man in a rumpled suit of extraordinary brown and yellow pebbly cloth. They didn't know him. He smiled, "How do, nice crowd, isn't it?" Yankee.

"Yes," answered Ben, "You from Boston?"

"Yes, indeed, how did you know? William Goodwin," the stranger said and offered his hand.

Ben shook his hand. "Ben Hedrick and my father, John. I recognize your way of speaking. Lived in Cambridge for a while. Pleased to meet you. Are you a teacher?"

"Well, for the present. My fiancé says we'll have to go into farming to make a living. She's the reason I'm down here."

John put in that farming's a hard life. "Teaching's easier, ain't it, Bennie?"

"Well, Father, it is and it isn't." He nodded as Calvin Wiley approached. "Here comes a man who hopes you'll remain in the teaching business," he said to Goodwin. Wiley was wearing his sixteen years as State Superintendent on a furrowed brow.

"Well, hello, Professor Hedrick! We're happy our University delegate has arrived. His spectacles winked in the fading sunlight. "Evenin,' Mr. Hedrick," he spoke to John, nodded to Goodwin.

Before John could introduce Goodwin, Wiley was shepherding

them into the church. "Come on in and register," he said, "We want to get down to business as soon as we can."

Calvin Wiley was like a mother hen rounding up her biddies. He led Ben over to the table under a "Welcome Delegates" sign and spoke to a young man seated there. "Alf, this is Professor Hedrick from the University. He's been registered since August, so you can just give him a program."

Alf was not glad Ben was there. His glare said so- and the rising color in his face. When Wiley had walked away, Alf muttered something and pushed a program at Ben while looking at Goodwin behind him. Ben decided not to notice the rudeness, but his stomach lurched anyway.

"You go on up front and sit with the teachers," John said, giving Ben a little push. "I'll sit over there with the folks that's just looking on. And Bennie," he added, placing a hand on his son's sleeve, "don't let the slavers scare you." He walked away quickly.

The church auditorium seemed smaller than he remembered from the time he'd come to Mr. Clyde's funeral. The gaslights were new and flickered bravely along the walls and in the chandelier hanging from the high ceiling. He saw that down the aisle past the spectators, the pews were marked with white ribbons and almost filled. For delegates, he supposed, and stopped at the first ribboned bench.

A fortyish woman with a cross expression moved the border

of her wide skirt a fraction of an inch to give him foot-room. He introduced himself, and she looked even more cross and replied with only "Humph." The black bonnet in front turned quickly so that wide eyes could stare at him.

He couldn't believe it. He was anathema. The "Defence" had come before him and scorched his way. His stomach took the news hard and tried to climb into his throat. His mouth was a dry as desert. He directed his eyes straight ahead without seeing anything.

Too bad these rude people didn't read *The New York Times* too. Then they would know Benjamin Hedrick was considered in the North "a noble-minded and patriotic scholar." A lot of good that does me down here, he thought.

Standing behind the pulpit, Calvin Wiley, with his earnest face, called the North Carolina State Education Convention to order. Then he stepped back after asking the minister of this church to pray for the Lord's blessing on this gathering. The preacher, a man Ben didn't recall, prayed, "May He who said, 'Suffer the little children to come unto me for such is the Kingdom of Heaven' be with your meeting. May He bless all who've come from near and far."

Ben added to himself, And protect the one from Chapel Hill who has tried to speak the truth.

Next Mr. Wiley introduced a Mr. Erwin from Mecklenburg and said he'd been gracious enough to agree to act as secretary until officers could be elected. Mr. Erwin, who was given to clearing his throat every few seconds, stood from his seat behind the long table and called the role of delegates.

By this time Ben was in dread of having his name set before these people whose disapproval he felt as a frozen solid quantity. But he knew it was coming. "Miss Eliza Froem, Miss Susan Harold, Professor Benjamin Hedrick..."

There was a sibilance, not loud, but quite definite, as if a flock of geese was heard over the water at a distance. When Ben answered, "Present," it grew louder. Mr. Erwin quickly called, "Arabel Howell."

Ben moved his right foot, then his left, crossed his legs, and shrugged his shoulders a little. Then the black bonnet turned around far enough for the mouth below the wide eyes to ask clearly, "Why don't you just leave?"

The hostile eyes were answered in his mind by Ellen's loving, anxious eyes. If she were here, he'd have to restrain her from slapping the face in the bonnet.

He didn't have to sit where he wasn't wanted, and so he found himself on his feet walking toward the rear seat where Father sat.

What was going on at the church door? He saw a whole crowd out there; it seemed about to spill in from the vestibule. What in the world? He was beginning to panic. After he'd sat down beside his father, he realized he'd pulled the hood of his cloak partly across his face. Am I a coward? He dropped the hood and sat there with burning face.

The crowd had voices. He heard: "Hedrick," "Which one is Fremont?" "Awful little man!" Sounded like some of them were children.

Ben prayed for courage and reminded God that all he meant to do was to tell the truth about what slavery has done, about what he, Ben, believed was right. He remembered his question to George at the depot and felt what it is like to be in an un-free place. These raving children! Taught by their elders to fear and to hate what is different. Deliver Johnnie and Charlie from such a fate!

Now Mr. Wiley was proceeding with getting the convention organized. Ben now felt quite detached from the activities. He and Ellen had talked about the possibility that there might be some trouble but they'd never conceived of such goings on. Why, it was hard to hear what Mr. Wiley was saying, although he went on and on as though he didn't notice the crowd at the back. Finally, the meeting was adjourned for the night, and Ben and his father moved with the others toward the door.

"Here he comes! Hedrick! Where's Fremont? Traitor!" The crowd of mostly children and youths seemed to be made of ugly open mouths and eyes glittering in the gaslight. But a path opened for Ben and John, and, emerging into the dark, they realized why.

In front of them at the foot of the church steps was an effigy, a man-sized stuffing of hat, coat and pants. Hanging in front of the apparition was a transparency on which was written, "Hedrick, leave or tar and feathers." Then a flame shot up; fire ate the effigy and the sign.

Ben thought he might faint. He had never faced a hate-filled gang in his whole life, and it was very frightening.

A hand grasped his upper arm and he jumped. "Come with me, Ben," Mr. Rankin said. Leaving John behind, he guided Ben to an alley down which they sped to the Rankins'' school, also their home. They got inside and closed the door before the crowd caught up. Ben felt not only scared but also a little ashamed. It was a long nightmare. Oh, to be at home. Ellen wouldn't believe this.

Sitting in the Rankins' back parlor behind tightly drawn curtains, they could still hear the sickening "Three groans for Hedrick." The sound was a lot like people vomiting. Ben felt a little like vomiting.

"I'm sorry, Benjamin," Mr. Rankin said. "If I'd had any idea there'd be a threat of violence, I'd have advised you not to come."

"Here you are, Ben, drink this chamomile tea," said his kind-faced wife, coming in with a cup. "You've had a bad shock. Oh, I hope those hoodlums don't step on my boxwoods. How many of 'um do you reckon are out there?" Mrs. Rankin babbled on, nervous but always the lady.

Ben was recovering himself. "You folks are so kind. Believe me; I wouldn't have troubled you like this for the world." He looked into the hallway and saw a dozen pairs of eyes peering at him. "Hello, young ladies," he said, "you are looking at that terrible person, Professor Hedrick. I'll try to restrain myself."

Giggles.

"All right, girls," Mr. Rankin addressed them, "everything is all right. Some of those chaps around here got pushed into a mean frolic. Just go back to your rooms; they'll go away soon." He smiled a very slight smile, his eyelid working rapidly.

"Mrs. Rankin," said a tall girl in a flowered wrapper, coming a little way into the parlor, "those roughnecks knocked your geranium pot off the porch and prob'bly broke it. Boys! I think they're mean, 'specially that Billy Land-he was one of 'em, I saw out the window."

Mrs. Rankin was refilled with housemother power and replied, "Never mind, Bertha. Everything's going to be all right. It appears to be that we can all thank the Lord there wasn't more broken tonight than a pot of geraniums. Run on to bed now, girls."

Ben sipped his tea, sat back in his rocker and closed his eyes.

Mrs. Rankin left the room so the men could talk.

Jesse, his old teacher, looked at Ben and said nothing for a while. Then, "You'd better stay on here for tonight, as we'd planned, but it might be safest to get out of town before daybreak."

"Yes, Mr. Rankin, I realize I won't be able to attend the rest of the Convention. They don't want me, that's plain. Why, my being there tonight just about broke up the whole thing. I'm real sorry about that. Will you tell Mr. Wiley for me? I just had no idea folks would be that worked up. Do you think they all read my article in the *Standard*?

"No, of course not. Our paper here didn't run it but did run cries of alarm at the black Republican in the University. Jim Fulton was telling in the Post Office he might have to get his boy away from Chapel Hill before he gets dangerous ideas."

"You two are my old friends. Ellen thinks a lot of you too. I know we don't agree on what's to be done about the slaves, but at least we are fellow Presbyterians so there must be a lot we agree on. Anyway, sometimes the head and the heart take different views."

"Benjamin, you were one of the very best students I ever taught. It was a teacher's dream to see how you responded to the world of knowledge opening up before you. Didn't hurt you were 'most twenty years old. We are so proud of you, of what you've accomplished, being a professor and all.

"If only you hadn't published this testament of yours. You must have known it would cause all kinds of havoc, even though none of us guessed it would come this close to violence. I mean that was an ugly mob. Must have been over 200; even if they were mostly young chaps. I am ashamed for them."

Ben drank the last of the tea. "Mr. Rankin, I didn't guess it would cause such trouble. I guess I was silly to think we live in a free country, even in the South."

"Yes, maybe you thought you could still speak out against the established customs, like you were still in Cambridge. We're not that open here because we've got to guard our world against the likes of those lying abolitionists. If we don't, we'll see the Union broken apart."

"I knew we were pretty defensive in the South, but I guess I'm learning how defensive. In Heaven's name, Mr. Rankin, can't you, a minister, see that we should not try to extend this sad system into new states?"

"But you see, Ben, I don't agree that slavery is a sad system, as you put it. The Negroes are descended from Ham who cursed God, and they are meant to serve the masters who are over them. Why, even the Apostle Paul baptized a slave; we're following his example. How would all these Negroes have heard about the Lord and accepted Him if they hadn't been brought to a Christian country as slaves? Millions have been saved!"

"Maybe they have, but then again maybe what they see in their Christian owners makes them want to find another way. We don't know that really. But all I'm saying really is that new states in this country built on freedom, states such as Kansas, should not be saddled with slavery. They should have a choice by ballot."

"Well, what you said almost got you hurt tonight, Ben. We don't agree on this, but I'm concerned for your safety." Mr. Rankin took a big watch out of his vest pocket and laid it on the table. "Let's see, as I was saying, you better stay here out of sight...until...There's a freight train stops here to load cotton bales, pulls out about 4 a.m., heading north."

"Yes, that would be good, Mr. Rankin, I'll slip down to the station and get aboard. It'll be stopping at Lexington so I can get off there and walk out to my brother Adam's house."

"Good, Ben. I'm sorry this happened. I'll let your father know. Feel I should apologize for most of the folks of Salisbury; they wouldn't want to see you hurt."

"Well, Mr. Rankin, thank you, but it can't be undone. I don't mind saying I was hurt, inside, but now I feel even stronger about saying what had to be said. I was surprised, but I see more clearly that slavery has bamboozled us into slighting a lot of important things such as education."

The grandfather clock began to speak from the hallway. Ben counted eleven echoing strikes.

Polly Rankin spoke from the doorway. She looked exhausted.

"Mr. Rankin, don't you think we'd better let Professor Hedrick get to bed? He must be worn out. He can sleep on the settee; here's a quilt and pillow."

"Yes, dear," her husband agreed. "It's hard for Benjamin and me to let each other go. I do enjoy matching wits with him, always have. But you're right, he should retire. He'll have just a few hours to sleep."

Polly left after saying good-bye to Ben and sending love to Ellen.

The two men stood. Jesse Rankin was half a head taller than Ben, but their eyes met to mingle thanks, admiration, and regret.

"All right then, Benjamin, I'll look in on you to make sure you awake in time to catch the freight."

"Thanks, Mr. Rankin, thanks for everything."

When the older man had gone upstairs, Ben took out his case and wrote to Ellen of the evening's disaster and of his plans. He would see her on Thursday, if all went well. It was so strange, after the uneventful visit he'd made to the Fair. He signed, "Good bye and may God bless you, my love."

Before going to sleep, Ben prayed in gratitude for deliverance in the form of Mr. Rankin. The black hole of recalling his firing from his work sucked him in then. It was a darkness, but not despair. He dreamed of climbing a ladder to the top of a wall. He climbed and slipped and climbed and slipped.

The big old house settled into silence. The student-maidens slept in their hair-papers. Mr. and Mrs. Jesse Rankin slept after whispering late. And Professor Hedrick climbed and slipped in his dreams.

Chapter Twenty-Five

Chapel Hill
October 22, 1856

Ellen was cold deep inside as she thought of Ben at the Education Convention. She wondered if his father would come. She paced the parlor, thankful Johnnie and Charlie had gone off to sleep.

Ben, Ben, my darling, she mused, if only you were right here with us. Ever since your account came out in Holden's paper, there's been trouble. I blame King Billy for putting you in this spot. Everybody knows he was just looking for a scapegoat for the Democrats. They'd lie down and die right now if Colonel Fremont got on that ticket.

Right now, I don't care about any of it, compared to the way I care about my precious husband. Why doesn't everybody admit he's a wonderful man? I know he's right about the Free-soil view. Most of our friends in Cambridge felt the same way. Seems as if a person's not allowed to think down here...

What was that noise?

Someone was coming across the deep front lawn. More than one. They were talking loudly. She couldn't pick out the words yet. Should she put out the lamp? Yes.

She sat in the darkness while many shoes crushed the fallen leaves.

She heard laughter, sounded like a lark, really. She remembered being a part of the crowd that had skated this place when it was a lake instead of a lawn. Ben had that drained. He was so smart. And so far away right now.

Now the strangers were actually on the front porch. Somebody played a fife, and somebody else beat on a pot or something. Then they were singing or screaming. Her skin shivered.

"Oh, don't you remember sweet Ben, Ellen dear..." Thought they were funny. Mean and funny. She felt tears rolling down her cheeks.

Thank you, Lord, the babies haven't wakened. Song over, the intruders crunched away. She dried her cheeks with her pinched handkerchief. Just students looking for a way to let off steam. Thanks, Lord, we're safe.

She blew her nose and listened to the silence.

When silence had prevailed for some minutes, Ellen found a match by feeling in the table drawer and fumbled to light the lamp again. The bitter smell of kerosene oil seemed sweetly normal. Then she wrote to Ben and the Rankins and told him about what had happened and that she was afraid he might be mobbed in Greensboro. "Keep well and trust in the great right," she advised.

She doubted that he would receive it, but the next day she wrote again. Putting down her thoughts made her feel better. Governor

Swain had come over today, but somehow that didn't keep her from feeling like an outcast. Where were their friends, now that the dismissal seemed definite? The Phillips, the Mitchells, and, for that matter, Ma? They knew she was alone and suffering but didn't want to get polluted, she supposed. Then she felt mean.

She reached out for what positive aspects of the day she could find. Mr. Watson and Mr. Loder told her at the store that they were on Ben's side. They say the Union will be dissolved if Buchanan is elected. Governor Swain came over to see the follow-up editorial in the *Standard* and said you had the advantage since you could prove the statements about your being supported as a student were falsehoods. The Governor said too he'd take pleasure in doing anything for me and that you should call on him if he can be of service.

Ellen bit the end of her pen and let herself wonder just whose side Governor Swain was on. He acted mighty broody. Seemed as if he spoke for the Executive Committee yet he had gone to bat for Ben by raising the question about the Committee's power to dismiss a faculty member.

She expressed her anxiety to the extent of writing that she wanted Ben home so they could talk and she could sympathize on "matters and things."

Letter finished, she tiptoed in, carrying a lamp to look at her beautiful babies. Johnnie, so relaxed in sleep, so intense when awake.

Love for him filled the sad spot in her heart, soothed the bruise of a threatened future. Charlie's fair curly hair made him look like a little cherub even asleep, and his blue eyes when open completed the resemblance, she reflected. The little sweethearts, what would their future be? Or maybe first of all, where will their future be?

> Davidson County, N.C.
> Oct. 22, 1856 (p.m.)

My dear wife,

It is now just dark, and I am at Adam's. I came to Lexington today on a freight train, and walked out here. Adam is going with me directly to take the cars at Lexington; I will go to Greensboro, where I expect to stay 'til tomorrow evening. They made a good deal of disturbance on my account in Salisbury last night, tho' they did no damage except to frighten pretty badly the women folks at Mr. Rankin's. The outbreak was much worse than any that occurred at Chapel Hill. Father was with me, and if they had made an assault upon me there would have been pretty rough times. After the attack I thought it would be useless for me to remain any longer, as it might excite the people still more. In fact I have come to the conclusion that it would be folly for me to make any further attempt at pacification. A good many people in Salisbury are very friendly towards me, but those who are against me are perfectly mad. They have not read my letter and will not read it. Mr. Rankin is very much afraid that the days of the Union are numbered, and it would be so were the same state of things existing all over the South which there is in Salisbury. If there were some harmless means of making the disunionists come out and show themselves they would be scared at their own insignificance. The danger is that by continual clamor they will produce a state of things, which will lead to final alienation of the different sections of the Union.

I expect to leave Greensboro in the cars tomorrow night.

Good-bye, may God bless you my love,

Chapel Hill, Oct. 23, 1856

When Ben came walking in the house Thursday afternoon, it was just after Ellen had read his letter about the ruckus at Salisbury. She was still trembling with the fear that had seized her on reading of the danger that her beloved had faced.

Their embrace almost mashed little Charlie. Ellen set the child down and flung her arms around Ben. "Oh sweetheart, are you all right?"

He met her eyes with his everyday calm blue gaze, threw his cloak over a chair, and kissed her deeply in reply. He felt whole again, and the Salisbury insult of sight and sound faded. They clung for a moment out of both need and passion.

Ben felt tugging on his pants and looked down into Charlie's pretty face. "Da," Charlie said, grinning.

The back door banged and the whirl was Johnnie, who assaulted Da's legs and ears too. "Papa! Papa!" Ben laughed for the first time in days and the family laughed together.

Ellen went out to the kitchen and asked Melie to take the boys outside for a while. Thank the Lord Ma had sent Melie over today, a sign Ma was softening toward Ben, too.

When Ben had told his story of what had happened and how he escaped the mob, Ellen was stunned. "That is almost unbelievable, Ben! Your own hometown or almost."

"I know, and poor Father saw the whole thing. We left him behind when Mr. Rankin whisked me off to the school, but I know Father suffered. He has always been so proud of me- a college student, and then professor- I expect he had me on something of a pedestal. And he has to see me practically ridden out of town on a rail."

"Yes, honey, I'm sorry for your father too, but I need to hear more about how it made you feel and what's to be done. Governor Swain was here..."

"He was? What did he say? Please tell me exactly."

Ellen pushed a stray wisp of her pale caramel-colored hair away from her face. Ben liked it when her thick hair escaped from the tight bun in which a young matron must keep hair confined. "Well," she said, "he talked about Holden's latest blast–the one making you out to have been a charity student, the University's charity, here and at Cambridge."

"I'll have to see that. All lies."

"That's what the Governor said; you wouldn't have any trouble setting the facts in order. He sounded relieved that Holden had put out something about you that could be denied."

"How did he act, Ellen? Friendly or not?"

"He was friendly, but to me it seemed like he was holding back, like he was feeling sorry for me, for us. Now, he did offer to do anything he could to help. Maybe part of that was feeling sorry for me being alone here with the boys. This was before either of us knew about what happened in Salisbury. 'Spose you didn't get my letter I sent there to the Rankins, but I said I was afraid of you getting that kind of treatment in Greensboro. I just had the town wrong. Anyway, are you really all right?"

"I'm all right, Ellen, but it felt just awful, I can tell you." He gave big sigh. "So Ol'Warping Bars didn't talk about the Executive Committee dismissing me?"

" He didn't deny it either, but he said he'd gone to bat for you by raising the question about the committee's power to dismiss a faculty member. And you can be sure I showed him that wonderful article in the new *Tribune*..."

Ellen handed him the paper, pleased she had found good medicine. He read aloud: "Notwithstanding the despotic rule of Jacobinical terrorism which just now holds fourteen states of this Union in the most abject servitude, it is not to be supposed that the fire of liberty is entirely shut out at the South, or that the self-constituted thirty tyrants--be the number more or less--by which each of these unhappy states is now governed, can long maintain their usurped authority. It is not credible that Washington, Henry, Jefferson, Madison, and the other patriots of the Revolution can have left no descendents behind them..."(2)

"I'll get you some lunch," Ellen interrupted. "I expect you haven't had any," she said as she headed toward the kitchen.

"What...Oh, thanks. I say," he called after her, "that fellow Greeley can spin a cocoon a words all right. I think he's going to come to me soon, is he?"

"Oh, he is," she said returning from the kitchen with a plateful of chicken and rice. She set the plate on the table beside him. "Here, you

eat and I'll read you the good parts. You'll feel like it's all worthwhile."
She licked her lips as if ready to savor a delicious tidbit.

"...it is impossible that there should not be in the South a strong cohort of those who do not bow the knee to the Baal of slavery, and who are wistfully watching for the restoration of the true and ancient worship of their fathers..."

She interjected, "And then he says something about the ticket. 'We have no recollection that any attempt has been made here to prevent the nomination and support of a Presidential ticket.'"

"Well," Ben said, "That's exactly what's going on in North Carolina. The Powers That Be did not permit the Republican nominees to be on the ticket. And I, Ben Hedrick, am the fatted calf being slaughtered as the sacrifice." His voice rose.

"Ben, you aren't eating."

"How can I? But I like to hear you read Grecley, so go ahead, I'll try. Good chicken." He took another bite.

She continued. "But if the friends of free political action in the South...('That's us,' Ellen inserted and Ben nodded) have a greater ferocity on the part of their opponents to encounter, so they may be supposed to have a much greater strength in themselves...And they have, besides, another great advantage, in powerful outside support. With the whole power of the Federal Government to sustain them in the vindication and exercise of their rights, in addition to sympathy of the entire North, it is evident that they occupy an impregnable position..."

"That's not us," Ben said. "My position seems anything but impregnable."

"Yes, my darling," she said softly, "but you know, I'm hearing a voice saying that if all those who oppose us are so wrong~I don't think they're wicked, just wrong~maybe we don't belong here." Her eyes filled with tears.

Ben took her hand. "We're going to fight to stay, but it makes me feel secure to hear you say that. It means that no matter what happens we're together. And Ellen, we both know life is easier and freer in the North."

"Yes, it's just that the North isn't home. I have thought about schools probably being better there for the boys. But let me go on with Horace, he's encouraging."

"He talks about hopes that the South will throw off the yoke of slavery by reverting again to the views of Washington and Jefferson, and instead of putting its weight into extending slavery into the new territories, will invite the aid of the North~('Well, I can't imagine that')~..."In some scheme by which with due regard to the rights and interests of all parties, those states, instead of giving new extension to this curse, may be able to rid themselves of it."

"Now we come to the good part." "That such ideas are not yet totally extinct at the South, that the crows have not yet succeeded in devouring all the good seed sown by the patriots of the Revolution, nor the great enemy of mankind in sowing tares enough to choke out the wheat, is evident from a letter which we publish today in which one of the professors of the University of North Carolina at Chapel Hill responds to an attack upon him by a Buchanan journal of that state as a Black Republican. If very few persons at the South have at this moment the intrepidity to confess, as Professor Hedrick does, their views on the subject of slavery, it cannot be doubted that a large part of the most intelligent, and most patriotic even of the slaveholders themselves fully sympathize with these views..."

Ellen paused for a breath. "This sentence must be a record for length--even for Greeley."

"This body of men to whom, in spite of the storm of Pro-Slavery fanaticism which now sweeps over the slaveholding states, we may look with hope for the return of these states to a better condition of intelligence and feeling, and for their ultimate deliverance from that terrible nightmare which hold them now in such a state at once of conclusive terror and paralytic helplessness."

"Exactly," Ben said. "We are in a nightmare and if people don't wake up, we won't waste many tears at getting out of it. Did I say that? But what did Governor Swain have to say about this when he read it?"

"Well, to tell the truth, Ben, he didn't say anything. He took the paper with him, and then sent it back by Dr. November."

Ben folded his napkin and stood up. "Think I'll take Johnnie for a little walk. I need to rest my thoughts and feelings."

"Do that, my love. I'll be all right, no daytime riots."

"I know, I know. Give me some of that healing balm." And they embraced for a long tender moment.

Ellen knew Ben could hear later about what had gone on here while he was enduring his fire.

Chapter Twenty-Six

Chapel Hill
October 24-November 5, 1856

This was the day he would pack up the lab equipment so carefully brought from New York. The hope-filled enterprise was over until some less troublesome professor of Agricultural Chemistry could be hired. Governor Swain had asked him to box the equipment. Phillips and Mitchell would complete the term with the science of their choice. So much for "Farming Becoming one of the Learned Professions", as in June's Commencement Address.

He couldn't yet stop thinking of this college world as his. Ben stared out his study window, glad of the rain streaking the morning gray. Gray was the color of his mood. No hurry to get over to Smith. Just as well to go later when most of the students would be in class.

Sitting down at his desk he reread Holden's crowing words in yesterday's *Standard*.

> "We learn that at a meeting of the Executive Committee of the Board of Trustees, held at the Governor's office on Saturday last, Mr. Hedrick was unanimously dismissed from his place as a professor in the University of this State.

"We make this announcement with much gratification, though we felt sure from the first that such would be the action of the Executive Committee.

"Mr. Black Republican Hedrick may now turn for consolation and support to his abolition brethren in the free States. His whole conduct in this matter has been not only in direct opposition to the best interests of the University, but it is marked with the grossest ingratitude; and he has shown, by holding on to his place after he had been notified that his usefulness was gone, that he is insensible to those impulses and considerations which never fail to operate in a high-toned and honorable man. Informed that he had ceased to be useful, he begged for time, and at last had to be dismissed..."

Now that really hurt but what followed was perhaps even meaner and was completely false.

"...Mr. Hedrick, we believe, is a beneficiary of the University; and he was sent to Cambridge on a salary and sustained there while acquiring and perfecting his knowledge in Agricultural Chemistry. Warmed into life on the hearthstone of the University, the viper turned upon his Alma Mater and upon the State of his nativity with his envenomed fangs..."

Ben heard himself make the strangest sound, the sound of a laugh and a sob in unison. He read on:

> *"...But he has been cast out, and is now powerless for evil. If the abolitionists should take him up, the history of his conduct here will follow him; and they will know, as he will feel, that they have received to their bosom a dangerous, but congenial and ungrateful thing."*

He balled the paper in his hand and threw it into the corner. Then he rushed into the parlor calling, "Ellen, I'm going to Smith now."

She came from the bedroom. Had she been crying? "Your coat, Ben, I'll get it. Must you go in the pouring rain, love?"

"Yes, I might as well tend to the burial rites. Thanks," he said, taking his cloak from her.

"And the umbrella," she handed him one of their prize possessions brought from Cambridge.

A quick kiss and he was off.

Chapel Hill,
October 28, 1856

While Ellen was settling the boys for the night, Ben sat at his desk to complete some correspondence before leaving tomorrow.

In a way the letter he'd written Governor Manly didn't make any difference now, but he was going to send it because he wanted to explain himself. Somehow it still mattered that he be understood-- even after being misjudged so harshly. He reread the letter written on October 14, another age.

Chapel Hill,
Oct. 14, 1856

Dear Sir:

> *I am glad that the Executive Committee did not yield to a popular clamor and remove me from my station here. For I believe that if I can have a full and fair hearing before the Trustees, the answer implied in the resolution which you passed will be found to be more than my offence merited, though as matters now stand it was as little as I could expect.*

> *No one more than myself acknowledges the justness and propriety of the usage, which prohibits members of the faculty from agitating topics relating to party politics. But there are times when it seems the usage may be disregarded. In fact, about eight years ago, one of the ablest and most learned professors in the University thought it incumbent upon himself to define his position upon the slavery question. But the principle circumstances which I would*

plead in extenuation of this breach of well known usage is the manner in which I was attacked. If members of the Faculty have their hands tied they should be shielded from assault. I am a citizen of the State, a native if there is any merit in that, and have always endeavored to be a faithful law abiding member of the community. But all at once I am assailed as an outlaw, a traitor, as a person fit to be driven from the State by mob violence, one whom every good citizen was bound to cast out by fair means or foul. This was more than I could bear. It seemed to me that I ought to resent it as a tyrannical interference with the rights of private opinion. So that in judging my case, it will be necessary to bear in mind the gross insults contained in "the charges brought against me in the Standard." What I had said here about voting for Fremont amounted to almost nothing, as no one expected an attempt to form an electoral ticket would be made. In fact I heard an influential citizen say that he would vote for Fremont himself if he thought that the electing him would bring about dissolution of the Union, whilst I would vote for him to make the Union stronger.

But the state of the case which comes home to the Trustees more directly than any other is the influence of my course upon the prosperity of the University. My own opinion is that if the newspapers will let the matter rest it will soon be forgotten. The election will soon be over, one of the candidates will probably be elected, and the others will soon cease to be talked of. What I said about slavery is neither fanatical, incendiary nor inflammatory. I have never held abolitionist views. If my reasons for keeping the increase of the slave population at home are good, of course no one will blame me for setting them forth. If my reasons are unsound I have erred in a question upon which there has always been, and probably always will be, an honest difference of opinion among thinking men.

But I am not disposed to find fault with the action of the Trustees. Some of the newspapers are pretending that I am only wishing to be dismissed in order to attain to profitable martyrdom. If I were base enough to resort to such a miserable trick my denying the charge would go for nothing. I do not believe however that any such charge will be made by anyone at all acquainted with the circumstances which placed me in my present position. I had not sought the election from the Trustees, and yet the appointment was most acceptable to me. When I graduated I took a subordinate position in one of the

268

Scientific offices of the General Government, a place not at all subject to the proscriptions of party. My services were so far acceptable that I was promoted at the end of the first year, and at the time I resigned my position my salary was equal to that offered me by the Trustees. It was against the advice of some of my best friends that I made the exchange. I have always acted on the principle that a good citizen will serve his native State in preference to any other. And I thought the situation offered me by the Trustees was one in which I might find honorable and useful employment, and at the same time do something for the good of my native State. Whether my labors here have been successful I will leave for others to determine. For my own part I am sorry that I have been the occasion of trouble for the Committee. But I hope that when they come to know me better they will find me to be one not deserving to be driven from the State by hue and cry.

Very respectfully, your obedient servant,

B.S. Hedrick

The two-week-old letter had a double edge when reread now. He took out a fresh sheet of paper and quickly wrote a few current lines to Manly:

"Accompanying this I send you a letter which I wrote

*before visiting you in Raleigh. I believe that I mentioned to
you the fact that I had written it; certainly I mentioned it to
some of the Board. When I came home from the Fair it was
too late to send it during that week, and the speedy action
of your Committee left no place for it afterwards. I send it
to you now and for your private reading, and as giving me
the opportunity to thank you for the uniform kindness you
have always shown me. I would send it to the Committee
as I at first intended, but for fear that it might come to
Holden and thus give him another opportunity of accusing
me of "begging."*

*"By Holden having access to everything the Committee
did, your first resolutions came to me in pretty much this
shape, "Resign or be damned," and that is what Holden
calls occupying a "delicate position!" Very delicate indeed!!
Something like giving you a delicate hint to leave by kicking
you downstairs. I am sorry some members of your Board
have such a fine perception of delicacy.*

*I thank you again for all your kindness. You helped cut
off my head but I know you made the blow fall as lightly as
you could.*

Truly and sincerely yours,

B.S. Hedrick

Chapel Hill
October 29, 1856

At the last minute, Ellen changed her mind and accompanied Ben to the stage. She had thought she couldn't bear for their parting to be public but found instead that it was unbearable not to be with him. The observant eyes of onlookers weren't her concern as he kissed her and then kissed little Charlie in her arms. He stooped to kiss Johnnie whose hand was held firmly by Melie. His blue eyes wrapped them all in his loving glance, which still held a sort of dazed incredulity.

To shouts of "Good-bye" he got into the muddy stagecoach with the three passengers who'd already taken their seats. The driver mounted his perch, slapped the reins and the horses began the trek down Franklin toward Durham.

"Let's go, Melie," Ellen said as soon as the driver had called to his horses.

After she'd gotten home and had her cry, she realized she'd forgotten to pick up the mail. Melie looked at her pityingly when she emerged from the bedroom and willingly started out up the street again toward the post office. "Lawd, Miss Ellen, we ain't thought 'bout no mail today, is we?" she'd said, and she went off carrying Charlie and letting Johnnie run before them.

On the return of the trio, Ellen took the *Standard* and quickly determined what Holden was doing to Ben today:

"*We are informed by a friend, who deeply regrets and strongly disapproves Mr. Hedrick's conduct, that we are mistaken in our belief, expressed in our last, that he was a beneficiary of the University...*"

Now he apologizes with Ben already leaving, carrying such hurt.

"*...We learn that he was in early life an apprentice to the trade of a brick mason; and that his father, having given him the choice of an education or his portion of the estate at his death, he chose an education, and thus paid his own way at the University. We learn also that while at Cambridge he was sustained, not by the University, but by an office bestowed upon him by Gov. Graham, Secretary of the Navy at the time.*

"*We make these corrections cheerfully, as certainly we have no disposition to do injustice to, or to trample on, a prostrate adversary. His punishment is great enough, without the aggravation of unjust accusations.*"

Ellen could almost hear her heart race as if struggling to escape such insulting lies. Her face burned, but she continued to read:

"...Nevertheless, the University has not been injured. On the contrary, it has been strengthened, if possible, in the confidence and respect of the Trustees and of the people of the State-strengthened by the prompt action of the Faculty and of the Executive Committee. We say this as a citizen of the State...We have done in this matter what has been done solely from convictions of public duty; and these latter remarks are submitted, not as a result of suggestions from any quarter-for none have been made-but in justice to ourselves and to the course we have deemed it our duty to pursue."

The election was over and Buchanan and the Democrats were predicted winners, but all this had no meaning to Ellen now. She sat down to respond to Mrs. Rankin's letter of sympathy.

My dear Mrs. Rankin,

I am very sorry that Benjamin's presence in Salisbury was provocative of such an outbreak & more so that he should have been the cause of so great commotion for you & fear in your own household......

"How far ought we go in concealing our views of matters & things? I cannot tell from your letter what it is you *consider his error...He believes not-never has-in extending the curse of slavery over the whole land. If in writing, one of the Trustees has told him that any brave independent man would have done the same. A man, at least 'tis said, has a right to hold what political opinions he pleases. Is this right of suffrage a farce & our experiment in self-government a failure?*

Mr. Hedrick, I know, does not wish to be lionized or sainted. He is quite willing to remain a man. I call ourselves political exiles, driven from the state of our birth by King Billy Holden in the name of the great Democracy...

Benjamin left Wednesday evening for Philadelphia. He would have remained here longer but the winter is coming on fast & so it is necessary that we be settled sooner...

Ellen frowned at the many inkblots and splotches that decorated the pages. She wrote at the top, "I hope you will excuse my warmth. I cannot control my temper when thinking or writing on the subject."

She knew she would have to make a fair copy to send Miss Polly or be ashamed to think of her opening such a messy epistle. But she felt a little more relaxed after letting some steam escape.

What did any of this matter anymore? Ben was gone, and her heart was sad. She was alone, except for the boys, in the little house they had moved into with such joy and anticipation~

She recalled the day she had gone to watch the blasting of a stone ledge which held back rain and spring water. The stone had been blown into many pieces, and the water had rushed forward and been absorbed soon into the ground under the tall oaks.

Looking out at the front lawn now, Ellen thought Ben was dynamite in this troubled State. His honesty blew away the memories which had held back the expression of true feelings. Now all was spilled; she and Ben were going to vanish~as though they had never been there.

This was no longer their home. Where should they go? She prayed for guidance for Ben, so good, so cut off from his moorings.

Chapter Twenty-Seven

Chapel Hill and points North
October 31, 1856-January 6, 1857

"So now I can say I'm for Fremont and no danger of belling, as Adam called the meeting in Salisbury," Ben wrote Ellen from La Pierre House in Philadelphia. Thus began Ellen's interim of being present to daily life at home in Chapel Hill while living in spirit with Ben on his travels. His almost daily letters kept her in one piece by locating him so that she could share vicariously his experiences, weigh them for herself, and reflect her perspective to him. She pictured an angel of the Lord sent by her prayer, keeping up with trains with no trouble at all.

When he wrote November 2, he told of going to a party of literary and scientific men at the home of a Dr. Bache. In addition to a "magnificent fine supper" Ben indicated that his drooping spirit was nourished by the approval there, particularly from a judge from Louisiana who complimented him on his "famous letter." Ben began to take heart to the extent of deciding that intelligent men North and South considered the action of the Executive Committee outrageous. He thought he would get out "a pamphlet for the good people of North Carolina and the rest of mankind." She smiled to know the air of another world was encouraging him to see more clearly.

Traveling on to New York City, he wrote from the Astor House that he begins to be in a hurry to look for a home, that he wouldn't feel comfortable "until I am settled down quietly to work with Mama and the boys close to me." He'd like to stay in North Carolina, he wrote, if there was a "fair chance I could do so myself." What did he mean by that? "A fight for the sake of a fight, or for spite or revenge is what we'll not engage in." She agreed, and then was gratified to read, "May God direct us to the right place wherever that may be." She found more of his thoughts to require mulling over, but took them as optimistic. He wouldn't think of "making things appear as I would like them to appear"...and "The treatment I have already received shows me plainly that a good conscience is all I can call my own."

Her husband was actually a shy man, Ellen knew, and so she wasn't surprised to read in another letter written the same day that he was asked to speak but refused. He was eager to get to Cambridge and "set out on his voyage of discovery." Ellen thought he was already embarked.

New York
November 8, 1856

My dear Wife,

Yesterday evening I called on Greeley [of the New York Tribune]. Found him busy reading proofs. He talked a little but seemed absorbed in what he was doing. I noticed this morning's <u>Tribune</u> a little notice of my being there.

This morning I called on Bennett [New York Herald]. He's a grave preacher-like sort of man. About as much unlike I had expected as he well could be. We chattered together very agreeable for a few minutes.

Everyone says there will be no difficulty in my obtaining work. Greeley told me not to be in a hurry. Better spend more time and get the right place. I guess he was about right.

I am sorry Mrs. Rankin wrote so strong a letter. I think however it is explained by the fact that she lives there in a hot bed of nullification. Of course the people there will think that I must have expected to be turned (out) when I first said I was opposed to slavery extension. I wish such people would just ask people in other places, say in Greensboro & Chapel Hill whether they would have expected that being a Republican was anything much out of the way. But it won't do to talk of this.

Those who know me & this whole matter will do me justice. Those who are determined to make it appear to my disadvantage will do so in spite of anything that can be said. I have received no letter from you here, but hope to

find a lot waiting for me in Cambridge. I feel a little blue
sometimes, but on the whole I am pretty well. The chief thing
that perplexes me is the uncertainty ahead. How long will it
be before I can see Mama and the boys, and where shall we
go to next? So much depends on the steps now to be taken,
but God has always led me heretofore & I trust & believe He
does again.

Good night

B.S. Hedrick

Sometimes Ellen felt almost dizzy accompanying Ben by letter. It
was as if he had moved from an outer edge to the center of things.
Why he even visited the famous Colonel Fremont, the innocent
cause of their grief. And the Fremont's were having their own grief
now that he'd been defeated, so good luck to them. The account was
worth rereading.

New York
Nov. 8, 1856

My dear Wife:

I am still in this big town. I had intended to leave this
evening but did not do so. I failed to find Col. Fremont
at home this morning when I called to see him. I shall go
again shortly.

I have kept myself very quietly here. There was a little disposition to lionize me last night at the Republican head quarters but as I did not encourage it cooled off very well— made no speech. But they gave three hearty cheers for me. I thought that might be set down against the tin pan serenade at Salisbury. I would write more but try and see Fremont.

Well I have seen Fremont and Jessie too. I went a little after six, and the servant told me the Col. was at dinner. I left my card saying that I would call again in half an hour. I waited nearly an hour & went back. I was told this time to walk upstairs, which I did.

I had not been seated long when Mrs. Fremont came in. She appeared glad to see me & I was soon acquainted. Directly the Col. came in. He appeared rather grave but soon became more genial. We talked about a good many things, politics among others. Mrs. Blair of Maryland came in after a while. She is a talkative old lady—southern style. Mrs. Fremont is lively & a little caustic, says she is a Virginian but don't like Old Dominion much. I think you might get along with Jessie first rate. She asked me if I had a wife. Tomorrow morning, I have an appointment to go back to see Mr. Blair [Francis Preston Blair, later congressman from Missouri] as he was out tonight. Col. Fremont offered to help me in any way he could & asked that I should write to him from Cambridge.

The next day's letter continued the story of Ben's New York visiting.

I am still in New York but expect to leave in the eight o'clock cars tomorrow morning & get to Cambridge tomorrow afternoon. I called this morning to see Mr. Blair. Found him & Fremont together. Blair is one of the ugliest, long headiest men I ever saw. Looks like an editor and nothing else. Fremont begins to cheer up. There is one fact quite cheering him, and that is wherever an intelligent community is to found, there his vote was largest. Wherever ignorance prevails there his vote was small. But for the Irish vote, Ol' Buck would have been defeated. I do not think I should have been better acquainted with Fremont if I had known him for years than I do now after two visits. Lively and talkative but not frivolous in the least. Does not look very smart nor grand. In fact to see Mr. & Mrs. Fremont you can hardly realize that they can be the persons about whom everybody makes so much noise.

I am a little blue this evening as it is now a week since

I had a letter from you, and besides I have taken a bad cold which makes me quite hoarse. So that I must Doctor myself a little. I believe here at the North there is a necessity to have a cold sooner or later every winter. Last year I had worse than this time although I took very good care of myself.

I saw yesterday Prof. Ellet who used to be in S.C. College. He left because he could not stand the tyranny of negrodom. Leiber will leave S.C. in a short time for the same reasons. Ellet told me that resolutions were once offered in the S.C. Legislature prohibiting professors in the college from coming North except in extreme cases with the permission of two physicians. But the resolutions were not passed, although seriously debated.

I will write you again as soon as I get to Cambridge.

Good night my sweet ones.

She was pleased to get a letter with a Cambridge postmark. He wrote that he planned to stay in Cambridge while writing to all parts of the country about work. Kerr, his fellow alumnus, thought Ben should re-apply to the Board of Trustees but Ben didn't think there was any hope there. "If they would act like men," he wrote, "and not be bullied by Holden there would be some hope of gaining something. The only thing I could hope to gain would be the setting myself right before the people of the state."

He wrote that he was invited to lecture in Washington but would not be there, and that she should mention this to the Governor and see what he said. She knew Professor Peirce's reaction meant a lot to Ben who revered, almost, the brilliant mathematician: "[Prof. Peirce] says my letter will do me good with thinking men at the North viewed merely as a literary performance." Peirce thought Ben should be able to get a good situation and said "they would give me all the scientific backing I want."

Meanwhile, on Ellen's home front there was excitement she could report in the post-election fevers in Chapel Hill. On November 10 she wrote him of "excitement here over Negro rising." She said that students met and asked the police to examine Sam Morphis [well-known Chapel Hill Negro]. Many knives were found in the rock wall behind Dr. Cave's. Quite a crowd of Negroes came Saturday [November 8] to hear who was president and said if Fremont was elected, they were to be free to kill the whites and have one-half the land. It was frightening, but the fear was to come even closer.

Also on Saturday, she was frightened considerably by a serenade, she reported. She had let [Melie] go and was left with only Esther [her young niece]. She was awakened about 1:30 by leaves rustling; a man sprang into the portico. She saw a fiddle, and then dropped the curtain. There was one fiddle and "bones" which played a tune.

She was much relieved when they left. "Esther said I needed you here but I said I'd be more frightened for your safety than mine." Ben was touched by her comment that she didn't know why she was so frightened by the serenade.

More reassuring was the account of Father and Ma coming to visit for an hour. But they didn't invite her to return the visit so she would stay away until she was invited. She announced her determination to go out to see her father at Rock Spring "if it hails brick bats. I am bound to have one chat with him before I leave Carolina again. Ma kissed Johnnie. Father, I thought, seemed to think more of him than ever. He asked Johnnie when he was coming to stay with Willie & if you were well & where you were."

She concluded, "Charlie was sick last night, but looks so beautiful and lovely."

Ben felt sick himself after reading that letter. He hated what she had endured without him for protection, yet he knew she was right to think his presence would have aggravated the situation. He could only pray and continue to look for a job.

There was much to tell when she wrote the next day also. She let down her self-imposed rule to dwell on the positive and told him she was getting "dreadfully misanthropic," feeling alienated from old friends, "considered a sort of somebody to be pitied." She didn't "care a snap for the sympathy of but a few, but I would like that all acknowledged us as who knew the right and dared to maintain it. I fear to speak freely because I might be sorry afterward, but I want to let some of them know how very shamefully I consider the treatment of you." She wanted him to write an "Iceberg" for the *Standard*.

She has found there was trouble also in Wilmington about the Negroes. She believes that if Fremont had been elected there would have been a general massacre in the South. To add to the dreaded feeling, "An owl is hooting~a very ugly noise."

Some good news Ellen could recount was a letter from Father Hedrick, sympathizing and suggesting they settle in Newton (N.C.) where there was political toleration. She added, "Now there is a chance of staying in old Carolina & being useful." She suggests they publish a newspaper in Newton~"independent in politics & religion, a truly family paper cheap enough for everyone to take...It will be a sacrifice, but not of truth, honor, or principle."

She wrote, *"Dr. Mitchell asked me about you, touching me on the shoulder. The Governor says he never had anything hurt so badly as your going away."*

Ben's answer to this letter, from Cambridge, November 17, was that he suspects Holden is behind this "negro business." He hopes to stay away from North Carolina until "the rascality of the plotters might leak out," people see the deception, and "...that traitors and Arnolds were the Holdens and men of that stamp." He asked her to be patient with his delay. "A good Providence watches over us & why should we be faint-hearted or distrustful."

Nov. 16, 1856

Meanwhile Ellen was doing her part by being willing to go wherever seemed right. Charles Phillips had brought a letter from his friend Thompson Bird of Fort Des Moines, Iowa, which offered sanctuary to the Hedrick's. She offered to be ready "in double-quick time."

In Cambridge, there was trouble at the *Almanac* where Ben was doing star tracking in person rather than by mail. The agreeable Captain Davis was leaving for another assignment and this opened the way for interference from Washington. James C. Dobbin, Secretary of the Navy, was also a leading North Carolina Democrat and fervent antagonist of slavery extension. Ellen learned from Ben's letter of November 18 that Dobbin was furious against Ben and wanted to turn him out of the *Almanac*.

Ben saw this as also the fruit of Holden's plotting and began to make other plans. He thought of moving on West, saying, "I would rather forget Holden & all rascals than to deal with the cowards." By Saturday (the 22nd) he was "evidently dismissed...paid for Uranus work." He signed off, to Ellen's pleasure, "It is near church-time—so good-bye."

But she was saddened to know in her bones his dismay that this darkness had followed him to Cambridge where he had felt securely respected. She assured him of her longing. "Home is a cabin with peace & my husband and children."

She was glad he decided not to appeal again to the Board. "Dr. Jones says you were imprudent to think the common people could distinguish between a vote for Fremont and an abolitionist. He predicts that slavery will dissolve the Union."

"Someone stole the front gates," she reported. "If I don't get away soon I shall get old a year in a month." Miss Ione [seamstress] says, "They are laying this negro business to you, murderous times if you come back. Do arm yourself with a good revolver before you return."

It was all she could do to attend to the household affairs and have sewing ready for Ione, who had made a new calico dress and rejuvenated a satin and velvet bonnet for Ellen.

She'd like him to send her the December *Godey's*, and what about a set of furs if she was to go North this winter? " Johnnie needs a suit, don't forget. A breastpin, if not too dear" would help her make a good first impression. With such lighter concerns she hoped to make both of them feel lighter.

On November 27 Ben wrote that he'd been making many calls before leaving Boston. Professor [Henry Wadsworth] Longfellow and Josiah Quincy [political war horse and former president of Harvard] were among those receiving Ben's farewell visits. While there he was also putting out job feelers both in person and by mail.

He wrote from New York December 1; he continued job-hunting and planned to leave for Cincinnati on the 3rd. There were some possibilities there. From Cleveland the next day he told her he'd bought a fine cashmere dress, and was evidently discouraged about possibilities at the colleges there. "If I can find nothing else to do, I can write a book or lecture or teach in an old field [rural] school."

December was a particularly hard month for the reluctantly separated couple. Ben sounded a wistful note: "Tell Johnnie papa is at 'Nati.'" [December 6]. He thought he'd like to live there. The governor-in Columbus-encouraged him but made no offer. He mentioned that ladies didn't seem fashionably dressed either at the hotel or at church.

On December 9 he wrote from Cincinnati with no pretense: he was really homesick. Also Cincinnati's air was heavy with smoke and soot because soft coal was used. The next day he admitted to being discouraged in job-hunting and planned to move on to Detroit and Chicago. If he had expected institutions in the free states to open before him-as Swain and Manly had predicted-he was very much let down.

Meanwhile he was receiving equally frank letters from Ellen. Niece Esther left and Ellen couldn't help crying a little bit but no one saw. Brother Henry was staying the night. "I hate so much to leave Old Carolina forever, but if she refuses us, why then there's nothing else left, she will be the worse for it."

On December 14, Ben was evidently staying in out of the soot and thinking over his time in Cambridge. He supposed she had heard about his speech there. He was called on after someone else spoke and talked for about twenty minutes. His "remarks were approved by the moderates of all parties, but some of the ultra-antislavery men didn't like them." He wanted to see how it would be to "face the music." Evidently it was a satisfying experience because he concluded that he might become a lecturer, "which is very good business."

The next day he went to the Unitarian Church to hear Horace Mann preach "a dry sermon, ordinary." He had declined the offer to teach at Farmers' College because they couldn't live on the salary of $700 per year. He will leave for Chicago in two days.

"I hate so much to go away, everybody that don't know you believing you the ally of the Abolitionists. Holden ought to be sued for slander."

Ellen was still smarting and grieving and not dreaming of the extent to which in the future Ben would become allied with abolitionists. Her "presentiment" [or yearning] that they might settle in western North Carolina was also to prove unsound. She was suffering the rejection caused by her absent husband's conspicuous stand, yet she feared for his safety should he come to Chapel Hill. And so she talked to him about the turkeys in their poultry yard and how much trouble they were giving her by getting loose. She joked that she'd put them in the pot to be sure of them but that she'd need him to help eat them.

A sad note from Chicago told her Ben had no letters when he got there. It was very cold, and he felt far from home. Two days later he'd decided it was too cold to consider settling there. He would "start for home soon if he doesn't get a situation and start out again in the spring." On the 23rd he would head back to New York where he would make arrangements about publishing his translation of a French chemistry book.

Ellen spent a lonely Christmas without Ben, despite the company of the boys and visits with Ma and the others. She heard from Ben at Ann Arbor where he spent the holiday as the houseguest of Dr. Henry. He reported hearing a sermon which was "much more anxious to detach men from Catholic worship than to make Christians of them." An admission of his innate shyness~"You know how I always dread the making of acquaintances"~was followed by the observation that traveling had made him accustomed to it.

Next his lonely wife had a letter from Lake Geneva saying that he had been "entertained very handsomely there." A little resentment began to flare. She wrote that some say it may not be safe for him to return, but that she can't bear his absence much longer. How would the students act after vacation? The "rising" had made the feeling against Ben much greater, she wrote on December 30.

But in her eyes the tide soon turned. On the second day of the new year she wrote that she thought it was safe for him to come home. "The negro mania has subsided," she wrote on January 5, 1857.

How much longer would this separation last? Ellen's letter of January 6 was a clear cry for help.

> *My dear husband,*
>
> *Your last letter from Geneva was received yesterday-great loss of temper & spirits followed the perusal, which continued still this afternoon when it was greatest soon after reading yours from Schenectedy. I can't imagine why you want to stay in New York City so long. You have been there twice before, so I suppose you had seen everybody that was to be seen, had nothing to do but to make some definite arrangements with your publishers, so what can employ you five days there when I am wanting you to come home so much. I fully agree that it would be better to remain a week longer if anything can be accomplished, but I have been enduring that week already-have been looking for you ever since last Thursday and now to be put off till the beginning of next week-it is mighty hard.*

Besides next week the boys will be coming in very fast, and I wouldn't like for you to be with many of them coming from Durham. I would much rather you get home and let all the bubbling subside into calmness before the boys come. You can form no idea of the intensity of the excitement that has been in the land. So if you don't get here by Monday you'd better wait a week or so after the session commences, so the first chat of Negroes will have passed around. But I do want to see you so dreadfully bad. Last week I set Monday or Tuesday certain for you to return. Saturday's letter brought the certainty to Wednesday or Thursday and now today's letter makes it quite probable that you won't be here before Saturday or Sunday. How long before "the winter of my discontent shall be made glorious summer."

New Year's day I had a large roast turkey for dinner, intending to have Henry, Sis Lina, Aide, & Belle to help eat it, but Ma was still in the country, so they could not come & I thought too that maybe you would come as you had told me to have something good that day, but I had to sit down to it myself. It was very nice. The next day Sis Lina spent the day with me & helped to eat it. I had it for dinner every day since. Sent it from the table today. That was doing right well for one turkey. You wouldn't come while it lasted, you needn't be surprised if you don't get much to eat when you do come. Only if I know in time I'll have another one on the table—that is, if you promise faithfully to be here at the time.

I am here alone...Ma gives a party for the boys tonight so Henry hasn't gotten here yet, it is a little past eleven. Time I was in bed but I must wait till he comes. 11 1/2–I must go and lie down. Can't sit up any longer. Good night. "May angels guard thy slumbers...

Chapter Twenty-Eight

Chapel Hill
January-April, 1857

Ben was home by January 14, seventy-seven days after he had boarded the stage on Franklin Street. He had traveled more than two thousand miles in futile search of another professorship. Meanwhile the compromiser Buchanan was elected president, and blood was shed in Kansas over the extension of slavery. A new year had come. The people of Chapel Hill, both village and college, had been riled up and had calmed down. Ellen had wept enough tears to do a washing, Charlie had learned to walk, and the front gates at the Hedrick place had been stolen and not replaced.

He stopped for a moment in front of the house. The tall oaks stood vigil over the little house with the hexagon room; their pebbly silver trunks sturdy, limbs reaching up and out, a few pale leaves hanging on like old settlers for the coming babies to copy. Spring would call out the stored life within.

Ellen's face was Christmas, New Year's, birthdays--all candles glowing with fierce joy. Ben had to carry both boys, wrapped like scarves around his neck.

Melie rushed from the kitchen with beaming brown face and,

294

"Lawd, Mistuh Ben! Mistuh Ben! You home!" Her strong humming could be heard between the clanks of stove lids as dinnertime approached.

Two days later, out in Iowa, Grandfather Sherwood took pen in hand to express his sympathy and astonishment that "Intelligent men such as Trustees of a University could disgrace themselves and dismiss a professor that was faultless...But I hope and believe that their tyranny exercised over you will establish you somewhere North of the Mason-Dixon line where my beloved great-grandchildren will escape, measurably, the blighting curse of slavery."1

As winter dragged on, the former Professor Hedrick found the hours long. A new editor had taken over the *Carolina Cultivator*. A new professor, John Kimberly, Ben's classmate at Harvard's Scientific School, was at work in the laboratory Ben had set up. Ben let a little bitterness show in a job-seeking letter to Iowa. He wrote that Kimberly was "...expected to say nothing that would offend the powers that be," and he commented on the election of Holden to the Board of Trustees, "...the reward of his villainy in attacking me." Then his good nature added, "I will wait as patiently as I can for the coming of spring and by that time I shall know to what place to direct my steps."

"The powers that be" were not indifferent to the suffering of their sacrificial lamb. Governor Swain himself brought over the following sign of their intention of support:

University of North Carolina,
Chapel Hill, Feb. 7th, 1857

Prof. Benjamin S. Hedrick was graduated, with the "first distinction" in this Institution at the annual commencement in June 1851. Immediately after receiving his degree, he accepted the position of Clerk in the office of the Nautical Almanac, in which he was soon promoted to the place of Computer. In January 1854, he was placed by a unanimous vote of the Trustees in the chair of Agricultural Chemistry in this University, which office he continued to hold until near the close of last term.

The undersigned have of course had the fullest opportunity to judge of the ability and attainments of Prof. Hedrick, and have no hesitation in expressing the opinion that in both these respects he is entitled to very high consideration; and that in the departments of Mathematics and Analytic Chemistry he has hardly a superior of his age in this country.

D.L. Swain, Pres.   F.M. Hubbard, Lat. Prof.

J.T. Wheat, Rhet. Prof.   E. Mitchell, Prof.

Charles Phillips, Prof. Civ. Eng.

As he had written Ellen from Cambridge in November, the impromptu speech he had made there had not gone down well with the most ardent antislavery men. Now that he had time to reflect, he sat down at his desk in the study and wrote to the editor of the *Cambridge Chronicle*. To the charge that he had defended slavery, he replied that he was giving the good points of what is, not what might be, and "when you exclude men from all Christian fellowship because of slaveholding, you are not dealing in charity with your brother."

"Slavery has been content to be let alone--many of the wisest and best of southern men, slaveholders themselves, have justified the holding of Negroes in servitude as a temporary expedient. They acknowledge that it was at war with the whole theory of our government, that it was a grievous curse to all states in which it prevails, to avoid wherever possible, extinguish as soon as it can be done...

"Whilst slavery thus acknowledged all its evils and imperfections and seemed penitent, the world was disposed to be charitable...But now the whole subject has changed, Slavery assuming that everything belongs to it, is determined to break down freedom where it exists. Having now all the powers of the Federal Government in its control, it openly pretends to the world that slavery is the normal condition of mankind. The rights of slavery are paramount to all other rights. Slavery is now aggressive. If freedom is allowed in a few of the old states, it is only by the sufferance of slaveholders, and unless the free

States put themselves on their good behavior this courtesy will be withdrawn~Under this condition of things, what is the duty of the free people of this country~they should rise in their might and put slavery down before it puts them down."

Reading what he had written, Ben had a lift of heart. He had expressed the convictions which had been growing in him since he wrote the "Defence." Maybe they'd been growing much longer than that, maybe since his youth beside the bridge where slaves' chains had clanked. It no longer mattered very much what the neighbors thought. His dissent had earned banishment, but what was this happiness he felt?

Now we are free. Sprung free, we are off to another life where our political views have companionship. And, he smiled, where the progress of science goes forward. Just please, Lord, if I'm following you, lead me to a job.

I must share that with Ellen. The other side of rejection is being free to move on. She's been moping and trying not to show it. Packing up and leaving this house is harder for her than for me. And leaving her family hurts, even though Ma's been on the cool side lately. Selina and Henry and the little ones were still close.

The Presbyterian Sewing Society had a little farewell party for Ellen. On April 1 she wrote Mrs. Phillips, chairman, to express her thanks for the needle book, which she would always treasure as a memento of pleasant hours. She packed her very mixed feelings about this along with all the other feelings she was boxing up to take away along with the wineglasses, the tureens, the silver, and the ironstone dishes Ben had bought and brought home,

But as Ben and Ellen lay in bed on April 14, the night before their departure for New York, secret feelings were shared, tears mingled. Then there was profound thankfulness in being together. Trouble was darkness hiding the days ahead. But it was a darkness to enter together, and together they were possessed of a light which could not be overpowered.

Epilogue

Benjamin Hedrick's career as professor and scientist was killed by the early frost of being fired by the University of North Carolina. The brief notoriety of political martyrdom produced no substantial offer of a comparable position anywhere.

While the young family struggled to exist in New York City, two chemistry lab partners flimflammed Ben out of most of his savings. He taught and tutored high school students until securing work in the office of the Democratic mayor. This ended in 1859 when it was discovered that he was a devoted worker in the Republican Party as it geared up for the campaign of 1860. He distributed the IMPENDING CRISIS and befriended its author, Hinton Helper of Rowan County, N.C.

In the spring of 1861, Ben went to Washington with the horde of office-seekers on Lincoln's victory trail. After much difficulty he finally gained an appointment as a chemical examiner in the Patent Office where he would work for the rest of his life. Later as chief chemical examiner, he was credited with improving procedures so that applicants were treated more justly.

During and after the Civil War, the exile tried to help his native state. He carried on a tremendous correspondence with North

Carolina wives and mothers desperately seeking the whereabouts of soldiers--dead, wounded, or prisoners. He helped his brother John get a port authority job at Union-held New Bern. There was no correspondence with other members of the family for four years--But when Graham Morrow was killed at Gettysburg, an army officer got word to Ben of Graham's injury and Ben was with him when he died.

Immediately after the war, Ben was able to get an appointment to the Union Commission which was to gather first-hand reports on conditions in the defeated South. May 12, 1865 found Hedrick back in North Carolina where he visited Raleigh and Chapel Hill among other places. He stayed at Eliza J.'s, took her Graham's effects, and was ever after highly esteemed by that lady.

Power had reversed. Governor Swain came to call on Ben and to beseech him to intercede with the Federal Government. The University and the village were destitute after years of privation and the encampment of Federal forces. Holden met Ben on the street in Raleigh and apologized for what he had done to him.

In the early months of the Reconstruction period, Hedrick assisted Governor Worth by pushing President Johnson to sign pardons for the former rebels in North Carolina. He also attempted to serve as a member of the Constitutional Convention in North Carolina in 1868 but failed to be elected as Orange County representative.

As parents, Ben and Ellen Hedrick evidently succeeded in passing on some of their ideals. They reared eight children in the house on N Street, Georgetown. Johnnie became a Jesuit priest and an astronomer in the Georgetown Observatory. Charles became a patent attorney. Alice married Harry Olcott and brought up a family. Jennie operated the Washington School for the Correction of Speech Defects. William was a physics teacher, Ellen a librarian, Mary Elizabeth a teacher and Henry an astronomer.

No doubt Ben and Ellen must have reflected that the blooming of their children made worthwhile the suffering, which had moved the family so reluctantly from Chapel Hill to Washington. Grandfather Sherwood had predicted it.

Endnotes

Abbreviations

BSH- Benjamin Sherwood Hedrick Collection

DU- Duke University, Perkins Library

NCC- North Carolina Collection, University of North

Carolina, Chapel Hill, North Carolina

SHC- Southern Historical Collection, University of North

Carolina, Chapel Hill, North Carolina

UNC- University of North Carolina at Chapel Hill, North Carolina

Introduction

Sherwood and Hedrick genealogies;

Leonard, John C. *CENTENNIAL HISTORY OF DAVIDSON COUNTY.* Raleigh: Edwards & Broughton, 1927.

"Defence" from *NORTH CAROLINA STANDARD, Oct. 4, 1856.*

Chapters

Chapter 5: William Gaston's address: "Address Delivered Before the Dialectic and Philanthropic Societies at Chapel Hill, N.C., June 20, 1832," 5th Edition, Chapel Hill, 1858.

Chapter 6: BSH address taken from Senior Orations, 1851, NCC, UNC.

Chapter 7, 8.9: Letters are from BSH-DU.

Chapter 10: Blessing sung by Mary is from Collyer's *Parish Psalmody*, 1850.

Chapter 12: Letter to Mrs. Rankin, BSH, SHC

Chapter 13: Charles Phillips letter to his wife, Charles Phillips Papers, SHC

Chapter 18: An account of the Archbishop flap is found in the University Papers, SHC. Follow-up: in 1860 the Archbishop gave the baccalaureate sermon to great acclaim. Quotes from *THE CAROLINA CULTIVATOR*, v.1, no.11, Jan.1, 1856.

Chapter 19: Grandfather Sherwood's letter from BSH, DU, Aug.11, 1856.

Chapter 20: Editorial is from the *Standard,Sept. 17, 1856*

Chapter 21: Ben's letter was published as his "Defence" in the *STANDARD, OCT. 4, 1856.*

Chapter 22: Proceedings of the faculty committee are from J.G.deR Hamilton's, James *Sprunt Historical Publications*, vol.10, and no.1. Quotes from the *STANDARD*, Oct. 11, 1856.

Chapter 23: Letters and quotes of committee from Hamilton.

Chapter 25: Letters from BSH, SHC, and Hamilton.

Chapter 26: Letters from Hamilton.

Chapter 27: Letters from BSH, SHC.

Chapter 28: Quotes from BSH,SHC & BSH, DU.